About the Cover

Both the front and rear cover of Tales from the Oldest City were inspired by black and white photographs taken in 1902 of St. Augustine Bayfront and the St. Augustine Lighthouse.

The cover design, including digital illustrations of local landmarks was created by Jennifer V. Ricker, lefteardesign.com, winner of the 2003 PhotoshopWorld Guru Award for website design.

Tales from the Oldest City
St. Augustine

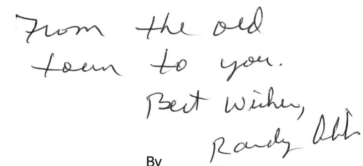

From the old
town to you.
Best Wishes,
Randy Abb

By

Randy Cribbs
Author of 'Were You There?'

iii

Tales from the Oldest City
St. Augustine

Copyright © 2003 by Randy Cribbs

Cover Design by Jennifer Ricker,
LeftEar Design

Published by OCRS, Inc.

Library of Congress
Control Number 2003111129

ISBN 0-9725796-1-3

Printed by United Graphics

Printed in the United States of America

To obtain more copies of this book, go to
www.somestillserve.com
or write
OCRS, Inc.
P.O. Box 551627
Jacksonville, FL 32255

Table of Contents
An Even Dozen

Ancient City Verse

Colorful Characters

Places

Secrets

To the great folks that grace the streets of St. Augustine, locals and tourists alike, for the pleasure I receive rubbing shoulders with you
And most of all,
For

AnnaJane and Eilis

SO LITTLE TIME...MAYBE

My meeting with Nathaniel Fuller started innocently enough. It was another one of those nights when I seriously questioned my sanity for the obsession I had with writing. I refer to myself as a writer not because I'm famous, or even widely published, but rather because I love to write. My published works include several articles for a variety of magazines; one book, though several manuscripts line my old worktable awaiting my re-look, re-write process. I write books for the love of it. I could wax philosophically and say it's good for my soul, or I have stories to tell. Or maybe putting pen to paper is the essence of capturing life and experience to share with the world. But that isn't really it. I just love it, and there's never enough time. Writing requires so much time, and there's much left to write about.

Because I need to eat, many of my days are spent on the silly little articles I write, or editing various documents for a variety of businesses and individuals. At the ripe old age of sixty four, I have become very good at this, but it's only a necessary evil, paying the rent while depriving me of precious time, too quickly running out, to write all those great masterpieces.

On that night there I sat, with time and no words. My obsession allows me to accept the occasional frustration, though as I age and time keeps passing by, I sometimes struggle to keep the panic level down. It's something I dwell on too much.

As I sat staring out the window of my loft off Avilles street, I could feel Zeke's beckoning, and as usual, I yielded to the call and headed the two blocks to my escape sanctuary.

Zeke's was a tiny, ageless bar just off the beaten path of downtown St. Augustine. One of those unique places where you could be among people yet be alone. I drop in almost every night. Because of its location, the clientele is primarily local. Very few tourists discover it and those who do usually lose interest when they also discover there is no band or jukebox. This situation is ideal because it feeds my need to think and reflect, yet the faces of regulars who gather give an inexplicable sense of comfort.

1

Entering the small bar, I took the only stool available, next to a familiar, mousy little man, perhaps forty two years old and ordered my scotch, the drink of any serious writer.

I nodded to the small, bowtied gentleman. His attire, as I had noted before, was about three decades out of style. He, too, was a regular patron at Zeke's, though we had never spoken. As a matter of fact, I couldn't recall ever having seen him speak to anyone. Like most of the Zeke locals, including myself, he seemed to have his own routine, always arriving at the bar about nine, drinking his wine until midnight or so, then departing.

"Hello," a soft voice said.

Startled that he had spoken, I nodded and returned his smile.

"My name is Nathaniel Fuller," he continued. "I see you in here frequently. Do you live near?"

"Robert Robson," I responded. "Yes, I live just a couple of blocks from here."

"Me too, about a block. I've seen you passing before."

How strange I thought; all this time, at least a couple of years, without a word between us in this place, and now Mr. Fuller seeks conversation.

We exchanged small talk for several hours. Turns out Nathaniel is a history professor at the small private college in town. He was obviously passionate about his profession and intrigued that I was a writer. Kindred spirits?

My first clue that there was something very different about this little man came when I asked how long he had taught.

"Oh, a very long time," he said.

"You don't appear that old," I said, "It must agree with you."

"Well you know what they say, things are seldom as they appear. I have been around quite a long time."

After that first encounter, Nathaniel and I talked often at Zeke's, usually small talk, though more and more frequently bits and pieces of our personal lives crept in. Sharing in that strange way strangers will often do. Things not readily volunteered to friends. Then one night, having left the bar together as had become our habit, I said goodnight to him as we came to his small apartment.

"Would you care to come up for a final drink before continuing your walk home?"

Another surprise. An invitation into the home of this private little man.

I was very curious, so I accepted and followed him upstairs. The apartment was very comfortable, filled with old turn of the century looking furniture, including a huge oak library table, filled with newspapers, magazines, and books. Conquistador type helmets and armor adorned the walls and rock fireplace mantle.

"Please excuse me a moment. I'll be right back." He disappeared into an adjoining room before I could respond.

Wandering around the ancient looking living room, I began leafing through the assortment of newspapers and magazines. To my amazement, several of the documents were really old, most with history making headlines.

"It's always interesting to see history as it was originally captured in print, isn't it?"

Startled by his return, I sputtered, "Yes it is." I turned to face him. "Some of these articles must be a hundred......" I could not complete my sentence. Nathaniel appeared somehow different. Not an old man, he seemed even younger, more vibrant.

"Something wrong, Robert?" he asked.

"You look so different," I stammered.

"Nonsense, let's have a nightcap."

I watched as he poured one drink into a nice crystal glass and handed it to me.

"I'll just sip my water," he said, lifting up an old scratched, but beautiful silver goblet. I could not take my eyes from his face as we discussed history and made small talk. He almost appeared to grow younger as he drank from the goblet.

"I love teaching history,'" he was saying, "Particularly history that I was there to witness, like much of that," he said, pointing to the pile of newspapers.

"Some of those papers are over one hundred years old. I don't see any less than twenty five or thirty years old. Where do you get them?" I asked.

"Well, most I purchased from the newsstands at the time," he seemed to catch himself, "Of course there are places you can get old articles," he finished somewhat defensively.

I watched as he sipped from the goblet. He seemed more relaxed, confident, with every sip.

"What an interesting looking goblet," I ventured.

Caressing the vessel, he said, "Oh, thank you. It's Spanish. I came by it quite by accident many years ago during my studies of early Florida. It changed my life and has become very special to me." He stroked the goblet almost tenderly. "You can feel the history." His eyes were jumping with excitement.

"Have you been a writer very long?" he asked, suddenly shifting the subject, as if he had revealed a guarded secret.

"Long as I can remember. Never enough time though. I'm sure as a professor of history you can appreciate that."

"Oh yes, the study of history is very time consuming. So much to read, research. Too much for one lifetime." He gazed thoughtfully at the goblet, the light dancing on its smooth, worn surface. "One needs so much time," he continued softly.

I couldn't take my eyes off the goblet. Though Nathaniel had been drinking from it throughout our conversation, it seemed almost full, its clear, watery liquid mesmerizing me.

"Oh, I'm so sorry," I said as I nudged my glass enough to spill wine on the fine polished table.

"Don't worry," he said, jumping up to grab a towel from the kitchen. "We'll get it right up."

As he scurried out, I picked the goblet up. It felt warm in my hands; almost comforting. I could barely make out letters on the well handled surface. D, then a small letter indistinguishable in the room light, then L e o...

"Here we go." Nathaniel returned and began wiping up my spill. He purposefully moved the goblet across the table, glancing at me suspiciously.

The mood had changed. I suddenly felt like an intruder. Our relaxed comfort level had changed abruptly, as if I had violated his confidence with my curiosity.

We both became uneasy. We tried to talk of other Nathaniel fondled the goblet and I tried, in vain, to keep n ~~~~ off of it. We were both relieved when I finally stood, thanking him for the evening, agreeing to see each other at Zeke's the next evening.

But it was not the same. Though we were not close friends, something had quickly developed between us. After that night it was gone. A crude type of one night stand, sharing secrets, then a frightening realization that too much had been revealed to a stranger; that motives and consequences were unknown.

We did see each other in Zeke's the next evening, but we were careful not to sit together. His manner toward me was suspicious at best. I felt awkward, almost embarrassed.

After a restless night, I decided to indulge myself with breakfast at my favorite Old Town eatery. After nibbling at the food and drinking far too much coffee, I opted for a leisurely stroll around town before starting work on a new article.

Not surprisingly, I found myself standing outside Nathaniel's apartment. He had left his living room window open and the curtains fluttered lazily in the morning bay breeze. I could not get my thoughts off the goblet, and Nathaniel. I scolded myself for the incredulous thoughts running through my head. Why was this strange little man so possessive of a simple cup? So much so, that it seemed to alter his appearance. Realizing the absurdity of my thinking, I reconciled my curiosity as writer's imagination. But what was it? What was his secret? Was it there, behind those curtains?

It was a week before I saw Nathaniel again. I had trouble finishing an article, so I decided to hit Zeke's early. Anyway, somehow I didn't feel as pressed for time lately. Nathaniel came in and took a stool at the far end of the bar. He looked tired, almost weary. I nodded and turned my attention back to the bartender who was regaling me with the Dolphins' prospects for the upcoming football season.

I could feel Nathaniel's eyes boring into me as I tried to hold up my end of the football conversation. I began to feel uncomfortable. The drinks didn't taste right anyway. Finally, about eleven o'clock I left.

An hour later, feeling refreshed from a warm shower, I decided to have a late night snack. Just as I was about to sit down there was a knock at my door. Wondering who it could be so late, I opened the door. It was Nathaniel Fuller. Seeing him close in the light was shocking. He appeared older, more frail.

"Nathaniel, good to see you," I said, not really meaning it.

"It's gone," he glared at me.

"What's gone? What are you talking about?"

"The goblet. My goblet is gone." He stared, waiting for a response, but I couldn't think what to say.

"Give it back. I must have it," he said with a frightening sense of urgency.

"Nathaniel, what are you suggesting? You probably just misplaced your cup." I was now more than a little irritated.

"No, no. I could never do that. All these years. It's a part of me. I feel so betrayed. Can't you see I must have it back," he pleaded, seeming to grow older before my eyes.

I felt sorry for the little man, but I also felt anger at his accusation.

"Nathaniel, I've had quite enough of this. I'm sure your goblet will turn up. In the meantime, I suggest you go home and rest. You look tired," I shut the door in his face, feeling guilty, but relieved. He knocked again but I did not answer.

I went into the dining room and sat down at the table where my snack was still waiting. Now very late, I thought about the new book I had been working on. Perhaps I should write a while, I thought, picking up the goblet for a sip, feeling the warmth of its liquid flow through my body with a tingling sensation. Nah. I'll write tomorrow. There's plenty of time....

***

TATTOO

Matt Cordova was shaking violently. He pulled the spotless hospital sheet tightly around his body and stirred fretfully as he slowly regained consciousness. A sharp stab of pain shot through his head and he moaned. A nurse was quickly at his side, gently forcing him back on his bed.

"Please, Mr. Cordova, you must lie still. You're in Flagler Hospital. The accident left you with a concussion and you have undergone surgery. Your wife was not injured; she's just outside. Do you hear me, Mr. Cordova?"

He was very groggy, grasping only fragments of the words she spoke.

"Accident? I don't remember an accident. I was with the hunting party. My wife . . ."

"Where is the village? How did I get here?" The effort of talking was painful and made him dizzy.

"Please stay calm, Mr. Cordova. The doctor will be here shortly." The nurse was soothing and slowly his memory awakened. The wreck? His wife?

"Where is Diane?"

Before she could answer, the doctor appeared, talking in a low tone as he shined a light in Matt's eyes and reassured him that Diane was fine. She would be in soon.

Memories receded and became mixed with dreams, no doubt the effects of anesthetics.

The doctor was speaking again. "You're very lucky. That was a terrible wreck. You have been very banged up, but your wife was thrown clear when the truck hit you."

Matt slowly remembered. Yes, it had been horrible and he was very lucky to be here at all.

The doctor's examination was over and he said, "Well, you seem OK, even though you have been running through the swamps with Indians for several days." He smiled.

"Indians? Several days? How long?"

"Six days. We had to perform surgery and you have been sedated

8

to help you rest."

Six days! He winced. As long as he was still his head did not hurt,
but with speaking came the pain.

The doctor said, "I'll send Diane in now, but only for a few minutes
and don't try to talk. You must rest, and if the pain becomes too
severe, tell the nurse. I have given instructions for a pain hypo, but
only if you ask for it." He smiled, "Don't ask for it unless you need it
and don't let the nurse suggest it; she has been captivated by the
story you've been telling in your sleep and might put you under to
hear more."

Diane's stay was short and he rested briefly afterwards, but then the
pain flooded back.

He moaned and the nurse was quickly at his side. "Are you in pain?"
she asked.

"Yes."

"Just lie still. The pain will be gone soon."

He felt the sting of the needle and the pain slowly slipped away as
he fell into a deep sleep. And the rain . . .

It rained in the swamps all the time, or so it seemed. Of course,
the smothering heat was just as bad. It had taken them several weeks
to get to this area from the fort in St. Augustine. They had stumbled
onto this village a few days before and after some tense moments,
determined the Indians to be friendly, though aloof. The Captain
ordered camp to be set up adjacent to the village to allow the party
to rest and regroup before continuing on with the surveying mission
the contingent had been sent to do in these godforsaken swamps.

The Indians, while not thrilled the soldiers were there, seemed to
tolerate their presence, though largely choosing to ignore them.

Cordova had seen Indians before around the fort, but never in the
wild. The contrast between the dress of the soldiers, in their heavy
clothes and armor, and the savages in loincloth--the women topless--
was remarkable. They were very dark and did not seem to be both-
ered by the oppressive heat and constant bugs. Their days seemed
to be spent hunting for food or repairing their strange little boats and
occasionally playing games with much laughter and animated move-

ments. Most of the soldiers were suspicious or afraid of the savages, but Cordova found them fascinating and took every opportunity to learn their ways and communicate with them, though he had made little progress in either area.

They were very clannish and took particular exception to any attention one might show their women. The women, however, were more than curious about these strange looking intruders.

The Captain was obviously concerned about their situation. On one hand, part of his mission was to record locations and status of any natives encountered, but to avoid trouble; very important since reinforcements were weeks away. Cordova understood the captain's concern, but in truth, these strange natives, well armed with crude weapons, far outnumbered the small surveying party and could easily have eliminated them at will, but so far, chose not to.

Any day now, Cordova was sure they would be continuing the surveying mission. He was right; partly.

Cordova was surprised two days later when his sergeant told him the Captain wanted to see him at his tent. When he reported, he saw that the Captain's aide was packing. Finally, thought Cordova, we're leaving. The Captain glanced at Cordova and came quickly to the point.

"We're leaving, but I want you to stay," he said.

"Sir?"

"We're breaking camp and continuing the survey, but you are staying back. I've ordered the quartermaster to leave you two months' supplies since our Indian friends don't seem too interested in sharing theirs. Your mission is to learn as much as you can about their tribe and document their comings and goings. The Governor is most interested in all tribal information."

"But, sir, why me? I don't understand!" exclaimed Cordova.

"Simple," said the Captain, "you seem to have taken an interest in them and I've noticed their interest in your hair."

Cordova had long blond hair, kept in a ponytail, quite a contrast to the other Spaniards and certainly to the dark haired savages.

"Besides, I need someone dependable and you've been with me since we landed and have served well. Questions?"

"Well, no sir, I guess not. But what if they won't allow me to stay?"

"That's why I'm leaving you. Proceed cautiously. Try to befriend them. I trust your judgment."

"Yessir, I'll do my best." But Matthew's mind was swirling. While he did find the savages fascinating, he wasn't entirely convinced he wanted to be alone with them. Well, anyway, he wouldn't have to continue the trek through the swamp; at least that was something.

Matthew watched, along with several Indians who had gathered, as the surveying party rode off. As they disappeared into the distance, he turned to find the savages staring at him with curiosity. He smiled, shrugged his shoulders, and began inventorying his supplies. The Indians lost interest and wandered off. One of the young boys remained and was watching him. Matthew handed him a musket ball, which the boy took and examined closely, then reached into a pouch and extracted a smooth stone, which he handed to Matthew. Just then an older brave yelled at the boy, who quickly turned and ran away. Well, he thought, at least that's a start.

Over the next several days, a routine slowly evolved between Matthew and the Indians, uneasy at first but eventually transitioning to a more comfortable situation. They obviously didn't understand why this stranger was here. The women and children seemed to find his presence exciting and went out of their way to observe his strange habits, though cautiously. While the males usually disappeared at sunrise on hunting and fishing parties, sometimes for days, the others stayed close to the village performing village chores. He noticed some males always stayed in the village, apparently for protection and, Matthew suspected, to watch him. Soon though, their monitoring became less obvious as he concentrated on learning their ways without being too intrusive.

When the young boys played and practiced their hunting skills, throwing crudely fashioned spears and shooting arrows at whatever targets attracted their attention, Matthew observed, laughing and clapping when a good hit was made. Soon, he began participating with them, much to their delight. Their enjoyment in showing off and teaching this stranger seemed to please the adults, who grew more comfortable with each passing day. His interest in the ways of the tribe slowly eased their suspicious view of him, though it was clear he was still considered an outsider.

As the days became weeks, Matthew became more obvious in seeking interaction with the males, feeling their acceptance was the key to tribal acceptance. Finally, he decided it was time to see where he stood.

There had been no hunting parties going out for three days, and all the males seemed to be engaged in making or repairing equipment associated with daily survival in the wild, working in small teams.

Taking the well worn trail leading from the village to the river where he knew several braves were building a large dugout canoe, he boldly approached the group.

They were chatting away as they worked; sweaty, tattooed bodies shining as they moved. As Matt drew closer, the talk stopped. He squatted by the boat and ran his fingers along the smooth finish, representing countless hours of work.

"Good," he smiled, using the tribal language he had picked up.

The braves stared briefly without speaking and went back to work. The process was fascinating. One brave tended a very hot fire. Another would scoop hot embers, place them in the dugout, and as the embers burned into the wood, others would quickly scrape away sections after which they would all begin smoothing the charred wood. As a fresh batch of embers was placed in the canoe, Matthew grabbed one of the tools and began helping them scrape. One of the braves grabbed the tool from him. His heart sank. He had gone to far. But the brave made a motion with the tool, obviously correcting Matthew's technique, then handed the tool back. He began scraping again.

After several hours, the braves abruptly dropped their tools and headed to the village. Well, thought Matthew, I guess the workday is over. As he got up to go himself, he saw that one brave had returned and was gesturing to him to follow. He did so and was led to a campfire, over which a large pig was roasting. A very pretty Indian girl pulled a piece of meat from the carcass and began eating, pointing toward the pig. Matthew looked around. A brave gestured to the pig, tore off a hunk of flesh and pointed to Matthew, who reached over and ripped a nice chunk off. The Indians sitting around the campfire all laughed.

This was the first fresh meat he had tasted in days since he was reluctant to shoot game, not knowing how the Indians would react. Fresh game was valued and he had noted respectfully that the Indians were very discreet in how much they killed, and where. Anyway, it was wonderful and Matt went to sleep that night very contented.

Sunrise found Matthew at the river once again, this time trying to spear a fish for breakfast, without much success. He had fashioned the spear from just the right wood, just as the Indians did, but had not quite mastered the art of throwing it. The Indians made it look so easy, he thought.

Suddenly, he heard a yell and turned to see a young girl frantically splashing out in the river. Matthew realized that she was in trouble and jumped into the water, working his way through the strong current to her. He reached the girl just as she went under and grabbed her hair, pulling her to the shore, where several women were jumping up and down yelling. They quickly grabbed the gasping girl and whisked her away.

He stood silently catching his breath, thinking what an ungrateful bunch. As he turned to make his way to his tent, the old man he recognized as the village chief was approaching, followed by two young braves and a woman, the same pretty girl who had offered him the pig. The party reached him and stopped. The chief said something to the girl, who handed Matthew a panther skin. As he took the skin, the chief placed his hands on Matthew's shoulders, said something and turned back to the village, leaving him standing dumbfounded.

Later, sitting in front of his tent, he was even more surprised to see the arrival of the pretty young Indian girl. She sat down crosslegged and handed him a bowl of food, which turned out to be delicious. He moaned with contentment and the girl giggled with delight. She stared at him as he ate. Suddenly she reached over and touched his long, golden locks. He sat still, indicating it was alright. She stood and more closely examined and felt his hair.

Though he was somewhat nervous, being unsure of the consequences should a brave see this girl touching him, he nevertheless was enjoying the exchange. Finally, though, as logic took over, he decided he had better end the pleasant encounter.

Rising to his feet, he stretched, yawned and turned to enter his tent. To his astonishment, the girl took his arm and pointed first to the tent and then to herself. Seeing his obvious dilemma, she entered the tent and gestured to him to follow--oh, well, he thought, guess at least I'll die happy.

Matthew awoke the next morning feeling very rested. With a great stretch, he crawled out of his tent to discover some sort of commotion in the village. Throwing on his boots, he dashed toward the excitement.

He was very surprised to see an old bearded man, draped in furs, standing in the center of a crowd of Indians, many of whom were touching his beard and laughing. To his further amazement, the man was talking their language.

As Matthew approached, the old man looked at him and said, "Well, you must be the Spaniard I've been hearing about." Matthew was excited to hear words he could understand after all these weeks.

"Who are you?" he asked

"Name's Castillo," he responded, "And I'm surprised to see another white man here. You should be honored these injuns let you hang around. What are you doing here?"

Matthew explained who he was and the trapper did the same. It seems he had been in the swamps for years just trapping and moving around, and over time had been accepted by the Indians.

Noticing a tattoo on his arm, identical to those worn by many of the braves, he asked what it was.

"Oh, that's a sacred sign for these folks. I'm sure I'm the only white man that has one. It's quite an honor.

"Why did they let you have it?" Matthew asked, his curiosity getting the best of him.

"Well, I saved the chief's life a few years back and the next thing I knew, they're holding me down, putting this thing on me. It made me one of 'em, kinda like the tribe's mark. Once a brave proves himself, he gets one, sometimes more than one. Different tattoos mean different things. You see a brave with a small feather on their right leg, that's real special. Not really sure what it means, but I do know it's reserved for something special."

Matt sipped his coffee, careful not to move his head. He had just finished his first meal sitting up and was exhausted. Diane helped him lift the cup to his lips.

"You're tired." Her voice was soothing.

"Yea, I guess a little. But I feel better. I don't think I'll need a hypo." He cringed at the thought.

"Well, the doctor would like you to taper off the medication anyway. Let me read to you. Maybe it'll help you to get to sleep."

He loved to hear Diane read; her quiet voice rising and falling with the words. There was music in listening to her, the words falling in a pattern as rhythmic as soft drums beating. He gazed at her long dark hair as she read. Her voice reminded him of something, or someone. . . the Indian girl. He smiled to himself as he thought of the dream. How improbable.

Hospital noises diminished, became obscure, and then were lost. It was silent and he was once again in the village.

The girl came to him again that night, and many nights after. It was accepted in the tribe. His days were passed spearing fish--he had finally been instructed in the art--and accompanying the braves on hunting parties. He looked forward to the evenings around the fire. Having picked up enough of their language to understand most things said, he marveled at their stories and the simple pleasures they shared. He was not sure how long he had been here, but he knew, with some remorse that the captain and surveying party would eventually return. He was right.

A week later, returning by dugout to the village from a fishing trip with two braves who had become good friends, Matthew was both excited and sad to see the Spaniards in the village. As he approached, they stared at him with curiosity. The sergeant-at-arms approached.

"Well, there you are, all made up like the savages," he noted, apprising Matthew's loincloth, sandals, and rainbow colored blouse.

The Captain's waitin' on you."

Matthew entered the Captain's tent to a quiet scrutiny.

"Looks like you managed to fit in."

"Yessir, they're wonderful people," he responded.

"Well, let's hear your report, then you can get your gear together. We leave tomorrow."

He delivered his report, recounting the cultural habits of the tribe, the areas they wandered, and their lifestyle. As he talked, he became aware of how close he had become with many of the tribe, one in particular. It would be difficult to leave, as if he had a choice.

Matthew finished his report and left to gather his belongings. The Captain seemed pleased. He was a good man, and a perceptive one.

With the sunrise, the surveying party was preparing to depart. All the village had gathered, most surrounding Matthew. The Captain watched as a young Indian girl took his hand and gazed softly into his eyes, tears swelling in hers. He touched her face, placed his hands on the old Chief's shoulders and turned to join the party. The column of soldiers headed out, but suddenly stopped.

At the rear of the column Matthew strained to see what was going on, at the same time glancing back for one last look at the village and the girl. Startled, he realized the Captain's horse was approaching him.

"Cordova," the Captain said, "I think I might leave you here a while longer. It doesn't hurt to have a friend in swamps. Is that OK?"

"Well, yessir, that's fine."

"OK then. I guess you won't be needing any of our supplies now, so we'll be off." He spurred the horse and trotted away.

Suddenly, he turned and headed back to Matthew, who was already en route back to the village.

"Cordova," the Captain yelled.

"Yessir,"

The Captain's eyes met his. "Cordova, I don't know when we'll get back down here, if ever. Could be a long time. That alright with you?"

"Yessir, yessir, I believe it is."

The Captain smiled. "Good luck, son." He turned once again and galloped off.

Matt was out of the hospital. All traces of the accident were relegated to the past. Back to work next week. But right now, he was watching Diane flit around, gathering things together for a trip to the beach.

"Oh," she said, throwing her long, raven hair back, "I bought you a new bathing suit. Try it on."

He tugged his trousers off and reached for the suit.

"What's that?" she said, looking at his lower leg.

"What?" he glanced down.

"There's something on your leg, like a small grease spot."

She was now in a crouch, examining his leg. He bent down to look. On his right ankle, about the size of a quarter, was a tattoo of a feather.

"I never noticed that before. When did you get it?" she grinned. "Are you an Indian?" she asked, smiling mischievously.

He looked into her dark eyes and touched her long black hair, seeing her face in the moonlight shining through the door of his tent. "We both are, he said softly, "in another time, another life."

Diane held his gaze for moment, then with a laugh said, "OK, chief, blond hair and all, let's go the beach."

* * *

RUSTY

Rusty walked slowly along the deserted beach, kicking through shells and debris the incoming tide had left. Every few steps he stopped to examine particular shells, or glass worn smooth by the interaction of sand and water. Many pieces found their way into the beat up bag he carried.

As the sun rose higher, he would stop occasionally and wipe his face with an old worn handkerchief. A few early risers passed him. Some spoke, but received no acknowledgment back. To Rusty, his endeavor was work. Unlike the tourists who frequented the beach collecting shells as souvenirs, Rusty's bag held the day's pay. This was his livelihood, one which he did grudgingly. To him, it was a day's labor, just as a factory worker who trudged in to the assembly line each shift.

Rusty drew near a crowd, all gawking and pointing toward the ocean. He mumbled to himself, without even a glance, "Stupid porpoises. People get excited about the most mundane things."

"Hey Rusty, how's it going." The greeting from a local surf fisherman enjoying a day off received only a grunt. "Looks like you got a good bagful today."

"It's alright," mumbled Rusty.

The fisherman turned back to his rod, thinking how lucky Rusty was, spending his days on the beach. Strange, but lucky.

No one knew much about Rusty. He had been in this area for many years but seemed to have no friends. Locals had started calling him Rusty because of his reddish hair and beard, now mostly white. He discouraged any attempts of those who would befriend him by simply ignoring them.

There was a time when his passing would trigger lively conversation among locals familiar with him. It was one of those conversation games, like talking about the weather, with each speculating about who he was, what he used to be. Over the years, his background had run the gamut from professional bum to frustrated CEO. Some stories, woven by the more imaginative gossips stuck, and there were many who would offer his biography up with such cer-

19

tainly when comments were made, that those who asked figured it had to be the gospel.

But in truth, no one knew. What was known was he kept to himself, rarely spoke, and seemed to enjoy the beach; he must, because he was there daily, like clockwork, strolling among the shells and flotsam, selecting treasures with knowledge and care.

One story had him an avid shell collector who had found solace in his hobby, which he shared with others through the gift shops on St. George Street. Two or three times a week, he would walk through the plaza to the shops to sell his wares.

The shop owners didn't know him either. They knew only that he brought nice shells, glass, small pieces of driftwood and never haggled over price, always accepting what they offered with a grunt.

Most of these proprietors were transplants who had an urge to be in this unique place with its history and magnificent beaches. Their little shops provided the income needed to enjoy the coastal community life. They were envious of Rusty that he apparently did not need to work and spent his days as he chose, perhaps selling his ocean treasures as a leisure pastime. Many wished they could be so fortunate to have Rusty's life, savoring the area as they pleased without job worries. It was a shame he always seemed so sullen, with such a life. It added curiosity to their jealousy.

As Rusty neared the end of his morning trek, he saw two tourists examining a shell they had found. They were thrilled over their find, a flawless black conch, rare in these parts, but had no idea what it was, only that it would make a great souvenir of their vacation.

"Do you know what this is," one asked, as Rusty approached.

He saw the shell and stopped. He looked at the shell and thought to himself, wouldn't you know it, a black conch. I could get more money for it than all the others I've collected today and these dummies kicked it up by accident.

"Just an ole' conch," he said. "I'll give you two large white ones for it." He searched in his bag and extracted a beautiful light colored conch.

"I don't know," the man said. "This one looks really cool."

"Oh give it to him, James, a shell is a shell," his female companion said.

"I don't know," the man repeated, "What else you got?"

Rusty stared at the man for a second and walked away mumbling to himself.

The man watched him go and said to his companion, "Friendly fellow." She laughed as they continued their morning stroll.

That's what I hate about this job, Rusty was thinking as he headed off the beach; always having to deal with idiots.

The bayfront café was crowded. The balding man behind the counter spotted Rusty as he came in and said, "Here's a place, Rusty," pointing to a stool at the counter. "I'll get your coffee and toast."

As the food was placed in front of him, Rusty searched in his bag and pulled a large unbroken sea clamshell out. "This OK," he said.

"That's fine," replied the man, taking the shell. "That's a real beauty." He placed it behind the counter. He knew the conversation was over so he turned to his other customers thinking, as he did frequently, that he should never have started this shell for coffee swapping. It had probably cost him a small fortune over the years. But, as with many rituals between people, it had become accepted as part of the normal routine, something to break up an otherwise monotonous day.

"What a lucky stiff," the café owner mumbled, "Spending his time just screwing around, while I sling hash. Some people have all the luck."

Rusty gazed out over the bay while he sipped coffee and munched his toast. Carriage drivers parked along the sea wall hustled tourists as they passed, allowing them to pet the horses, knowing it provided an opportunity to get a customer. He speculated on occasion that he could probably make more money by selling his shells directly to tourists, working this bayfront and the plaza. Unfortunately, that would mean dealing with all those people, and he wanted no part of that.

He finished his coffee and left the café. As the door closed, a

21

tourist at the counter asked, "What's that guy's story?"

The café owner glanced at Rusty walking away. "Been coming here for years. Never stays long. He's one of those lucky jerks that apparently doesn't have to work. Just spends his time walking the beaches, playing with his shells."

The tourist sighed, "Well maybe one of these days..." his voice trailed off.

Time to unload this stuff, Rusty thought as he headed toward St. George Street. Another day, another dollar, more of the same tomorrow.

His first stop found a crowded shop. Several tourists fondling various trinkets, making the big decisions about what to get for Aunt Helen and cousin Joe. The shop owner spotted him and said, "Lay your stuff out, Rusty. I'll be with you in a moment."

Rusty proceeded to a corner of the store and started carefully laying out his wares.

A well dressed customer, watching Rusty grouping his shells together by type, walked over.

"It must be wonderful," he said, "Having the time to collect those beauties. Strolling the beach, out of the rat race, enjoying the twilight years doing as you please in a hectic world."

Rusty abruptly stopped his sorting and looked up at the great philosopher. He picked up a shell. Some called it a double-sunrise. Two halves, like butterfly wings, perfectly matched. Except for colorful rays fanning out from the hinge holding the sides together, it had the same pattern, with a background of translucent white.

Holding the smooth, unblemished shell, he said. "How does this fragile perfection survive the breakers? Some don't. The most simple bump will cause them to split."

He picked up an oyster shell. Shop owners seldom bought them, but he always had a few. "This one," he spoke again, "On the other hand, fights to have a place on the rock it clings to. No two are alike. Small shells cling to its humped back, but it is comfortable, locked together in its own world." He looked at the double sunrise in his other hand. "The smallest storm will break this apart and then, separated, it will eventually splinter into tiny fragments. But this one,"

22

he continued, looking back to the large oyster shell, "Opens in its own good time, and then not even the strongest of storms will break it. Even those that wind up gracing all those driveways have a sense of permanence, another life."

He sighed and placed the shells back on the mat and stood. He spoke again, quietly, "We are all like one of them. We outlive desires, some sooner than others. I was not so gifted as I one time thought. Too many things were too hard to understand. Too many problems were beyond my scope. The beauty of that double-sunrise is temporary unless held captive, perhaps by you. We do not see the oyster as beautiful. It is sought after only for the meat inside, but that is not its spirit. The oyster is there," he said pointing to the shell. "Always there." The customer and shop owner, who had wandered over at the sound of Rusty speaking, stood dumbfounded.

Rusty turned to leave, then suddenly turned back to the two men. "Which one are you? Do your desires drive your life or is your direction pre-determined? Do you have a choice?" He made his way to the door and left.

"Wow, what was that all about," the customer exclaimed. The shop owner, agape at what had occurred said, "I don't...", he stopped, ran after Rusty yelling, "Rusty, you forgot your money."

But Rusty, leaving St. George Street toward the plaza did not hear, for he was already thinking about the next day and the drudgery of his work, strolling the beaches, searching for its treasures.

***

RIVERMAN

The gentle wind held the first hint of fall. Refreshing in the early morning; crisp, but not yet cold. Of course, it would seldom be truly cold. This was after all Florida; though north Florida, but still never what those further north, or west, would call cold.

Except for storms in this semi-tropical climate, the winds are a gentle breeze, gusting higher in late afternoons. The tops of taller cypress trees sway in rhythm with the gusts. These trees are truly a miracle of nature. Slender, irregular trunks, small, almost delicate appearing limbs and evergreen type needles rather than leaves. The smallish limbs probably a key part of nature's design; built to splinter in storm winds so they would not provide swaying leverage that could crack the trunk further down or uproot the tree from its foundation of water and mud, a requirement for good cypress growth.

At some point in their evolution these trees had adapted to the brackish water of the St. John's River, blending, and in several places where it was more marshy, dominating the abundance of flora and fauna that thrived in the tidal waters.

The St. John's, one of only a handful of rivers in the world that flows south to north, meanders through Florida 310 miles, eventually feeding into the Atlantic Ocean. Because of its brackish makeup, a variety of both salt and freshwater fish are found. Sport and commercial fishing thrive. Communities along its banks range from modern, gated condos to shacks on stilts or floating on barrels along the countless creeks and feeder streams that make up this unique waterway.

Cap made his home in one of those 'cracker' shacks. The construction of such a thrown together collection of discarded or dislodged material would never be allowed today. But forty years ago when Cap and many others threw these structures together, permits were a little known concept. Besides, most of those surviving the frequent storms were built far off the beaten path of the river like Cap's place, located about a mile into a feeder stream that merged into wetlands, accessible only by shallow water skiff; unless you wanted to brave the gators and moccasins for about one and a half miles through those wetlands to an old logging road. Only those who had been in the area a long time were aware of the shack's existence.

After its many years of sun, storm, and wind, Cap's shack contained few original boards. Normal deterioration, storm damage, and simple modifications constantly changed the appearance of the old wooden structure.

Cap made most repairs using an assortment of planks, lumber, and poles that routinely floated in with the tide, having been discarded or broken loose by storms, called flotsam by most. The pilings, which constituted the basic foundation of the structure, served to both stabilize the shack and keep it high enough to avoid the high tides and occasional flood. He had put the pilings in by hand. The trick was to get them through the two to three feet of mud and ooze into the harder sand underneath, called hardpan, and then another two or three feet into that.

Many of the pilings were cracked and had been reinforced over the years so that now much of the shack's walls were pole. When a piling became rotten or worn thin at the waterline from constant water action, another would be inserted along side, bolted or tied to the old to shore up the support. Not the prettiest construction job, but very functional and inexpensive.

Winding around the shack and snaking out in three directions was a boardwalk system put together from flotsam of every variety, including natural driftwood and splintered boards and planks. The walkways served to get Cap to and from his variety of old boats moored along the walk.

He had collected the boats over several years, most given him after storm damage by an owner who had no interest in the repairs required. All but one were 'shallow runners' which allowed him to pole through the marsh growth, cattails, and lily pads.

The one exception, a twenty-foot open fisherman, was kept anchored at the feeder stream entry in a small cove. One of the smaller skiffs carried him to and from the larger boat when he was crabbing or for his infrequent excursions to the nearest marina for dry good supplies. He lived a simple life, largely subsisting on what he caught and trapped. A shorthaired pointer and three cats shared his residence.

Murphy, the pointer, had been given to Cap as a big eared, ugly puppy, and his looks had not improved much in thirteen years. But he was a good companion and kept most snakes and varmints away. He also had never grown out of puppyhood and was fond of chasing about, splashing through the shallows and bogs after a variety of seen and unseen wildlife.

Having grown up on the water, Murphy considered himself part fish and part duck, which probably allowed him to move around the wetlands as easily as he did. His morning ritual, as Cap was having coffee, was a frolic around the perimeter, diverting in whatever direction and for as far as something that attracted his interest would take him.

Cap finished his coffee and while planning his day, realized Murphy had not returned; several minutes overdue. Very unusual for the chowhound. Cap decided he had better take a look. That's when he met Alice.

Alice Daley grew up in New England, the daughter of a successful lawyer and community do-gooder mother. An only child, she was raised amidst high expectations to follow in her father's career and her young life was directed toward the 'right' social circles. She tried to please her parents, doing well in school and participating in the requisite activities. To their dismay, however, Alice also participated at every opportunity in other endeavors to satisfy her tomboyish nature.

She was the recipient of many stern lectures when frogs, snakes, and other creatures were found in her room, or she arrived at home with cuts and scratches from jaunts in the woods or along the bay.

Alice tried to be a dutiful daughter, but her love for the outdoors and nature usually overrode her desire to meet parental expectations. Still, she tried for twenty years.

As she started her third year of college, pre-law of course, her grandmother died and left Alice a considerable sum of money and property, enough to make her self-sufficient. She immediately informed her parents that she was changing schools and her major to marine biology, her true passion. After much discussion and no consensus, the switch was made.

Now, nine years later, college and several years' experience behind her, she had finally gotten her own grant for a State of Florida project funded by the federal government.

The state was interested in developing a method that would encourage individual commercial fisherman to produce more softshell crabs. Their intent was twofold; first, when crabbing slowed down, most crabbers gillnetted to supplement their income. The gill nets killed or maimed several species of wildlife: turtles, manatees, otters, and such, so the legislature wanted to prohibit, or limit it.

Because blue crabs were a big industry and the livelihood of many Floridians, it was thought the cultivation of softshell crabs, currently monopolized by large fisheries with expensive equipment, might be the alternative to gillnetting for the smaller crabbers. Alice was to study and determine the natural contents of the river; salinity, indigenous organisms, trace material, and so on throughout the year and as a follow-on, provide input with others on possible ways to get crabbers more interested in softshells. Specifically, a process that would make it more profitable for them.

Blue crabs go through a shedding process called molting. Essentially, as part of the maturation process, usually spring and fall, they shed their hard shells with a new one forming as that occurs, not unlike a snake sheds its skin.

When the shells are still soft, these crabs are an eating delicacy, usually deep-fried. The key, however, is to get them while the molting process is occurring before the shell hardens; a process that can take hours or days.

The sign that a crab is about to molt can be seen on their back fins, called swim fins, two rear, flat, arm like extensions, different from their six jointed legs. The ends, and largest part of these extensions, the paddle, changes color from clear to translucent white to pink and finally to red; the sign the molting process has begun. The earlier in the process they are, the longer it takes to molt. The crab is very vulnerable in this state, as even the claws are soft and incapable of pinching. Many are eaten by fish and other crabs. So when they are caught, they must be protected, kept alive, and at the right moment put on ice for processing. A short, involved process.

For smaller crabbers, to simply catch enough softshells at the right time in the process to market is not profitable enough to warrant their time. But, if a way could be found to keep the crabs alive and protected throughout the process, without major investment, the crabbers would probably be willing to invest the time required. Good for fishing because of less gillnetting, good for the seafood industry, and certainly good for diners.

So on this day Alice was in her normal work state; up to her thighs in muck, collecting samples from a small feeder stream. Her problem at the moment was this loudly barking mutt currently in a yelping frenzy, after startling her into the muck and hyacinths.

"Murphy!" A weathered old man appeared and grabbed the dog's collar, pulling him back.

"Nice dog," said Alice facetiously, trying to regain her composure. "He always this friendly?"

"Well, he really is. Just not used to seeing people out here on his morning trek. I surely am sorry. Can I help you?"

"No, I just need to get these containers into my kayak and get rinsed off." She sloshed toward her small boat. "I'm Alice Daley," she said, giving Cap a small salute. "Currently, a muddy Alice Daley," she continued, appraising the variety of mud and vegetation dangling from her clothes.

"Cap," he said glancing at a nearby blue heron methodically stalking his prey. "I sure apologize for Murphy. My shack is just over yonder," he said, pointing, "If you'd like to rinse off and have some coffee."

Normally Alice was cautious about interacting with strangers in out of the way places like this and had noticed those strangers were often leery of outsiders as well. This time, her instincts told her Cap's apology and offer of help were genuine.

"Sure, why not. I'll follow your skiff in my kayak."

As they approached Cap's shack, she was having second thoughts, but his friendly conversation on the trip there calmed her concerns.

He seemed a quiet man. Probably not that well educated, but obviously very knowledgeable about the river and its wildlife. As he pointed out various birds or reptiles on the way, making interesting comments, he seemed to be talking to himself, enjoying their beauty as if seeing them for the first time. She added to the conversation sparingly, enjoying his low, calm narrative.

After a precarious walk down the rickety boardwalk, wishing for handrails, she found to her amazement the shack interior was clean and orderly, though sparse. What little furniture there was had either been handmade or repaired from whatever material was available. A small, simple propane burner served as a stove. A hand pump, over a sulfur stained sink provided water and a heavy looking insulated box obviously served as the refrigerator, though she did note the floor trap door containing a metal cooler; probably used during winter as cold storage, hanging in the chilly waters.

"Interesting décor," Alice remarked. "Looks very functional."

"Well, it ain't much, but it's more space than I need and I got 'bout all the furnishings I can use," he said, scratching Murphy's gray face.

Alice was impressed with the ingenuity and simplicity of the shack. It caused her to realize how many non-essential things most people accumulated.

"Here, I'll show you where you can rinse off while I get coffee going," he said, leading her onto the porch and a barrel type shower, around which a small privacy wall had been erected.

"Thanks, I'll just be a minute." This is gonna be cold isn't it," she inquired.

"Well, a little. Later on, when the sun heats the water in the barrel it ain't bad. But probably chilly right now," he seemed a little embarrassed.

"I'll be fine," she laughed. I was getting a little warm anyway.

"OK, I'll see you inside. Yell if you need anything," Cap responded, enjoying the young woman's attitude and company.

Later, over interesting coffee, Alice explained her grant.

"Yea," he nodded, "You can only catch so many mature softshells in the traps before they harden. Lose a lot. Sometimes ain't hardly worth it. Most of these crabbers can't afford lots of equipment, so the fix would have to be simple and inexpensive. I'll think on it."

Alice smiled at his obvious intent to help with the problem. This simple riverman contemplating matter of factly the solution for a problem hundreds of thousands of dollars had been thrown at. She did really like him though. Suddenly, she had an idea.

"Cap, would you consider showing me around the area? I need to take a lot of samples, record tidal flow, talk to crabbers, and so on, and it would really be helpful to know where I am while I'm gathering my information instead of spending time with bad maps and a compass. You probably know the fishermen and I could pay you a little." She waited for his reaction.

"Sure, love to. 'Bout all I'm doing for a while is running my trot lines and pulling a few crab traps. No pay necessary. Stay here if you like. Bring a little chow if you don't like lots of fish and crab."

She thought about her comfortable motel room. It was noisy. She could save lots of time by actually being on the river all the time. Besides, she really liked this sharp-witted old man. Easy to laugh.

"Well, are you sure," she said.

"Of course, no problem."

"OK, but I'll provide the food to supplement your fish. I love fish, by the way."

"Well I know every way there is to fix it."

That evening in her motel, while she selected the clothes and research equipment she would need, Alice thought about the situation that had developed. She smiled as she imagined what her upper crust parents would say if they knew she was about to become roommates with an old riverman, in the middle of nowhere. She realized though that she felt really comfortable around Cap and was excited about what she could learn from him.

She finished her packing, enjoyed a restful night and after her last warm shower and downy towel dry the next morning, she stepped out of the air conditioned, carpeted convenience of the spoiled and headed to Cap's world.

For the next several weeks she and Cap poled and sloshed through the wetlands, creeks, and tributaries of the majestic river. Cap knew everyone, or so it seemed. Very familiar with a large area of the river, Cap proved to be an able sample collection assistant. He spoke the unique language of river fisherman and their respect for him was obvious.

Alice learned to appreciate the skills of river folk as she helped him work trotlines, pull crab traps and cast net shrimp; though the cast net was more of a shawl around her until she finally got the hang of it.

The historical research Alice had completed about the St. John's fascinated Cap. Though he was very knowledgeable on the ways of the river, what he knew of its history was largely from stories. As they sat on the porch baiting trotlines to be set later, or cutting crab bait, she shared her knowledge with him.

He was particularly intrigued to learn that steamboats on the river were the main vehicles into central Florida during the late 1800's. Before roads and railways, travelers took the river: northern tourists seeking to regain their health in the subtropics, or merely warmth in the winter. Citrus and vegetables were shipped north. The St. John's was a long sanctuary when Florida was a strange and forbidding place.

"You know Cap, I really enjoyed seeing the pilings from that old steamboat dock yesterday," Alice now remarked. Cap had taken her to Coley Cove, a large indentation off a major turn of the river just north of Palmo Cove and Six Mile Creek. In the early 1900's a large dock snaked out into the cove from the eastern shore several hundred feet. It was said that folks came there by boat, then transferred to horse and carriage for the ride to St. Augustine for vacations or one of Henry Flagler's big affairs. Alice found it all very exciting and romantic and enjoyed sharing the information with Cap. "Oh, I go there all the time. Good place to fish around all them old pilings. Lose lots of hooks though. I guess from what you told me, it got lots of business with them steamboats up and down the river. Must have been something."

How neat it was, Alice thought, this old man who had been around here so long found her trivia interesting.

"River's calm today. 'Course it's always lazy," Cap said, as he finished carefully wrapping a trotline around its notched container.

"I've noticed a lot of the people around here call the river lazy. You know why it seems that way?" she asked.

"Guess I never thought about it," he replied, scratching his chin.

"Well basically, it flows incredibly slow because from its origin near Vero Beach to the Atlantic ocean at Mayport, the river only drops thirty feet-only six inches from Palatka to Jacksonville. That makes it one of the slowest rivers in the world."

"Well, I be dogged. That's something," he said, leaning back in his old porch chair, stretching his back.

"Look at that," Cap said, pointing to a river otter floating on his back, water glistening on his silvery chin and chest while he playfully cracked two river clams together.

"Used to trap those fellows," he said, almost sadly.

"Did you do a lot of trapping," Alice asked.

"Oh yea. Everything: gators, raccoon, possums. Everything. Didn't used to be any stores anywhere near here, so you really had to catch or trap 'bout all you had."

He sat silent for a moment, watching the playful otter.

"Those fellows live to play. 'Bout all they do. I don't trap anymore. Haven't in a long time. Really no need to. Ain't hardly worth it." The otter was watching them, knocking his clams together.

Alice suspected Cap's abandonment of trapping had more to do with his respect for nature than his 'hardly worth it' comment.

"Besides," he continued, "there's so much in this river, don't really need to waste time with the likes of these critters. Why, that big old sea bass you caught the other day ain't nothing." He glanced at her mischievously.

"A few years back I caught the biggest tarpon you ever seen right out there," pointing out to the river.

"Pulled me around in my skiff for four hours," he added.

"Well, I believe the tarpon part because I know there's lots of salt water fish in the river," Alice smiled, "but I'm not sure I believe the four hours."

"I swear it," he grinned emphatically. "Had blisters from the rod."

Such was the banter they enjoyed as they shared the beauties and secrets of the old river. The maidencane, willows, and sawgrass blending with stunted gnarled cypress trees further south, to the tall, straight cypress trees of the north river. There was always time to stop sample collections or trot lining to observe the feeding or antics of ospreys, kites, herons and Alice's favorite, the manatees. To Cap's delight, the first time they encountered a pod: two adults and three youngsters, Alice shed her shoes and slid over the side of the boat into the water with them. They both knew these gentle creatures, called sea cows by many, were harmless, unless you startled them and got run over. Nevertheless, he enjoyed her obvious enjoyment of the friendly beasts.

"Don't get to close to the mama," Cap had warned, as he nodded toward a large female, floating on her back while a small calf suckled at her belly.

"Don't want to interrupt mealtime," though Alice knew he didn't want her to accidentally get hit by the huge flat tail.

"Cap, you know these beauties eat up to one hundred pounds of water plants a day?" she responded.

"Knew they ate a lot. I give 'em lettuce when I have it. Seem to like it OK," he responded.

"Oh yeah, they should love it. They're true Floridians too. Don't like water colder than about forty-six degrees."

"I shore agree with that," he responded. "Kinda ugly to be mistaken for mermaids, ain't they," he said, referring to old mariner tales about mermaids that were apparently these large, lovable creatures. "But then, I guess the eye of the beholder...," his voice trailed off as he gazed out over the river.

"Yes," she smiled, "the eye of the beholder."

Cap's claim to know how to fix fish every way known to man proved to be correct. Alice watched in disbelief as he methodically moved about, chopping, dicing, breading and soaking combinations of fish or crab and spices, both store bought and self produced, many very suspicious looking, but also very tasty.

He had also never grown tired of fishing, and on this day, they had decided to take a break from the research and traps to enjoy a little sport fishing. They were working the marsh mallows, a beautiful pink hibiscus native, and the maze of other floating vegetation in search of the illusive, famous Florida big mouth bass.

Cap had been surprised at the deftness with which Alice used a spinning reel, but he had taught her much about landing a fighting bass once hooked.

Now, as usual Cap was working a 'lunker', river jargon for really big. He worked the bass up to the side of the skiff and also as usual, gently removed the hook while holding the huge mouth with his free hand. The bass sprayed water as it swam away.

"Cap, you never keep bass, including the few I caught. Why not, don't you like the taste?"

"Oh yea, they taste great. Used to eat 'em all the time. I don't know," he paused, "Don't seem to be as many any more. And besides, they are to the river what a lion is to the jungle. It's their place. They're king. Just don't seem right anymore to keep 'em."

There was silence between them for a few seconds.

"But," he laughed, "They're still fun to catch, ain't they?"

"Yes. Yes, they are, Cap," she responded, again marveling at the understanding and sensitivity she had come to see in this wise old man.

Cap was talking again. "Used to be lots more bass, but the state sprays all the time, trying to kill a lot of this hydrilla and stuff. Spray probably hurts the fishing, don't you think?"

"Well," Alice chose her words carefully, "There probably are some residual effects, but the spraying is really the only way to control these plants. If you let water hyacinths, hydrilla, and water lettuce go, it becomes clogged and then rots and drops to the bottom with the first frost."

"Looks like that would be fine. Gets 'em out of the way," said Cap.

"No, what happens is once on the bottom, the plants take the oxygen out of the water; oxygen the fish need, as well as other marine life. So even though they no longer clog the surface, where they also take oxygen, they do a great deal of damage under water."

"Well, I be damned. Didn't know that," Cap looked thoughtful. "I know hyacinths shore spread fast."

"Oh, they are the big problem. And you know they aren't even a native plant. They were actually introduced from South America by some ill informed visitor in the mid 1800's. One hyacinth plant left unchecked will cover an acre in one year. And there would be no oxygen under that mass; so, no fish.

"Guess the spraying makes sense after all. All this time, I figured they was just messing the fish up."

They sat enjoying the quiet for a while.

"By the way," Cap said, "Been thinking about your softshell problem. Probably a way to do it. Just need to play with it in my head for a while more."

"Well that's great, Cap. I really appreciate your help," though she was thinking she didn't see how he could figure it out if all the experts hadn't so far. "You have been a tremendous help already. It would have taken me much longer to gather my data without you. As a matter of fact, I have more than enough samples and information, and I really should leave in a couple of days. I need to start putting everything together in the lab, and bring in other people for input."

Cap sat quietly.

"I shore enjoyed your company. I hope you'll come back again," he finally said.

"I will, Cap. You can count on it. I'll leave you my address and I assume I can send you letters to the marina."

"Oh yea, they do that for me. Well, how 'bout some crab cakes?" he said, collecting himself.

"Sounds great. I'll do palm salad."

The days grew shorter as winter took over. Alice had been gone a couple of months and Cap's life had returned to his routine.

Approaching the longer walkway from his shack with the big boat full of traps to be repaired, he was looking forward to getting a fire going and getting warm.

He finished securing the old boat and realized Murphy had not arrived. He was usually there to greet him by the time Cap bumped the dock. A little worry crept in.

As he approached the shack, Cap could see that a lantern was on. Someone was inside. He opened the door carefully and peered into the flickering light.

Alice was sitting crosslegged on the floor, with a contented Murphy resting his head on her leg. A fire was going and a large turkey with trimmings was on the table, as well as a bottle of wine.

"Well, it's about time you got here. You hungry?"

"Well, I'll be..." Cap's surprise was overcome by his pleasure at seeing his friend again. "How are you, girl? You bet I'm hungry."

"Good. Let's eat and talk, then I have a surprise for you. I'm afraid I have to leave first thing tomorrow."

Cap's disappointment was quickly replaced with catching up on Alice's project as well as passing on news of his own.

"Well, I don't know 'bout you, but I'm ready to turn in," Cap finally said much later.

"Yea, me too, but first have a look at this. Had a devil of a time getting it into the kayak." She had walked over to a corner of the cabin and was pulling a large box out to the center. Cap had not noticed it earlier.

He grabbed a corner of the box to help her.

"What have you got here?"

"Well, open it up and see," she responded mischievously.

Cap could not remember when he had gotten a present. Alice was enjoying his excitement.

The box contained a solar water heater kit.

"I checked with the experts and they say this will work good in this area. But I'll let you set the panel on top of the roof." She watched him with a big smile.

"This is quite a gadget. It must have cost a lot of money. I don't know what to say."

"Say nothing, Cap. You were such a great help to me. But more important, you're a good friend. It's a gift for a good friend." She could see his eyes growing misty.

Alice quickly stretched, yawned, and said, "Let's turn in. Maybe you can follow me in tomorrow and we'll do breakfast at the marina."

"Yea, that would be good," a contented Cap responded.

Spring found Alice slaving away with the boring end of her project; office and lab work, and bureaucratic reports, so Cap's beat up post card was a pleasant departure.

"When can you come? Surprise for you," scrawled in his crude hand.

Alice thought for a moment.

I could use a break, she decided, and it would be great to see Cap. Mind made up, she started planning.

"Gave your crab problem a lot of thought," Cap said as they tied Alice's boat up a few days later.

"Come on up and have a look."

Cap led the way through the shack, out to the porch, to which a large extension had been added. Alice approached a maze of wooden boxes and pipe he had set up, all with water flowing through them.

"Got the idea from my live bait bucket," he said.

Alice still did not comprehend what she was seeing. What exactly was this contraption. Cap had built, out of treated lumber, a series of identical size boxes. PVC water pipe, drilled at short intervals ran through the boxes, creating an aerator/filtration process, leaving 3 or 4 inches of flowing water in the bottom of each.

"Course you have to move the crabs from one box to the next when they're ready and that's pretty much a 'round the clock operation. Guess anybody that wanted to do this would have to be willing to work. You can sort out the crabs when you pull the traps and even those real early in the peeling stage can be put in these things and finish molting without getting chewed up. I think if you could figure a way to add a little more salt water to it, they would do even better."

Cap waited for her response. After what he had done sank in, Alice said, "You put all this together and have been rotating the crabs by

yourself?"

"Yea, not too complicated. But like I said, a fellow doing it for a living would probably need to hire help at peak molting times to separate 'em out."

Alice's amazement was obvious. Sometimes, she thought, the answer is simple and we make it too complicated to see. This old riverman had put together a simple softshell crab process system, taking the crabs to maturity, keeping them alive, to be put on ice and subsequently frozen fresh and shipped. And he did it with boards, plastic pipe, screws, and braces. And it works!

Alice began to calculate the cost. This type operation could be as small or large as the operator wanted it to be. Which meant independent crabbers could start small and get larger as they earned and grew. Since most would have electricity, pump flow would be better; Cap had only water from the artesian well.

"Thought I'd return the favor."

She turned toward him, a puzzled look on her face.

"You know, for the water heater," he continued.

"Do you like it?" he asked anxiously.

Like it, she thought; simple material, built by the crabbers using it; no middlemen, very minor financial investment. She was already thinking simple modifications and applications.

"Yes," she finally replied.

"Yes, Cap. I like it. I love it!"

Favor returned in kind. Favor to a friend.

She looked into the old weathered face.

"Thank you, Cap."

***

THE ARTIST

George was an artist. One of many who graced the streets of the nation's oldest city. It was not particularly profitable; he could have made more money painting houses rather than canvas. And too, there were the rules to be followed: paperwork for city permits, which were given only for short periods of time, requiring routine visits to see the methodical clerk who took his job far too seriously. The permit was issued by areas, so one also had to be careful about where he set up, and on what day because during special events, and there were many, the city frowned on peddlers clogging the Plaza or streets most frequented by tourists. And the tourists. So distracting. Necessary, for the occasional painting they purchased, but still sometimes a pain. Often he wondered why he didn't do something easier.

But artists like George were stubborn and unreasonable. Traits necessary to produce from blank canvas that original, unique representation of the subject at hand. He derived much satisfaction from the knowledge that he created meaningful paintings of both old and new, living and inanimate, throughout the Old Town. He prided himself on his talent to mix oils and watercolors to just the right blend to capture the true essence of a particular scene or object.

George had come to St. Augustine about six years ago. His wife was dead and his daughter was married and far too busy with career and children to see him very often. He worked for many years as a department store manager, which allowed little time for the pursuit of his true passion, painting. After his wife's death, he could find no reason to continue his rather dull life at the store, so he quit.

His fond recollections of St. Augustine from a brief vacation three years before brought him back. He had rented a small room with private entrance off one of the old historic side streets downtown and was still there. He required very little money, and his meager savings, along with the occasional painting sale usually met his needs. If things did get tight, he would do caricatures of tourists in the Plaza, an undertaking he despised, but it was always good for a few quick bucks.

With his paintings, George had found a new passion in life. One that often caused him to regret the many years he had spent pursuing less meaningful things.

He had very few friends, discovering early on that too many so called 'artists' had some talent but little desire and were in constant need of money, which they would ask for without shame. Besides, there was little time for friends after the effort required to produce just the right mix of oils that would cause the canvas to come alive. The few young artists he did befriend shared his desire, over profit, to produce life on canvas. For them, he sacrificed precious time encouraging their true enthusiasm for the art itself.

To George, the mixing was the essence of a great painting. Over the years he had discarded many canvases because the mix just did not capture what he was seeking. Feeling that too many artists did not understand this, he allowed only those dedicated enough to that task to share in his quest.

In late March, that wonderful time of year in the Old Town, when everything just seemed so fresh and alive, George awoke to the steady pounding of rain on the tile roof of his old building. His room was one of four which had been converted from an old turn of the century two story house to make it worthwhile to keep as rental property for the owner. George had what he considered to be the best located room, on the back inside corner. This afforded much more privacy and was quiet.

He listened to the steady drumming of rain and hoped it wouldn't last all day, as sometimes happened this time of year. Anyway, the rain presented an opportunity to work on paint mixes, and hopefully, if it quit soon, he could catch the light just right while it was still wet to get a scene he had been after for sometime now. Catching just the right time and circumstances for some subjects was tough, and then getting the perfect mix to capture that combination of light and wet made it even more of a challenge; one which George lived for. There was a scene in the plaza he had been trying to perfect for years, but to date had not done so to his satisfaction.

Amazingly, at about eleven o'clock the rain began subsiding and then almost quit. George felt a sense of excitement as he watched the sunlight dancing on the wet foliage and surrounding buildings. Perfect, he thought, grabbing the paint he had just mixed and his old artist case.

He headed for the Plaza, which to his delight, was almost deserted, due no doubt to the rain which had now stopped completely. Moving quickly, he set up his stand and opened his new mixes.

With some nervousness, he spread a small amount on the corner of his canvas and grimaced slightly. Not quite right. "Damn," he mumbled to himself.

Slowly, he opened and stirred the other can and applied a portion on another area of the canvas. Disappointment was immediate. Oh well, he thought, not today.

"It's tough to get it just right isn't it?"

He turned to see who had spoken.

Standing before him was a young man and woman. With a twinge of annoyance, George thought, oh great, just what I need, a couple of know it all tourists.

Glancing at the paint cases they each carried, he said, "I beg your pardon."

The girl, whose hair was an extraordinary cooper-gold color looked at him through intensely turquoise eyes and responded, "Oh, please forgive us. You didn't seem pleased with the colors. Isn't it difficult to catch wet and light just right? We find that a challenge where we're from too."

"And where might that be?" George asked.

"Oh, far from here," she responded.

Something about the two puzzled George, then he realized what it was. They were both dressed alike and had the turquoise eyes.

The man, who had not spoken said "We don't mean to intrude, but as artists ourselves, we appreciate your disappointment in not being able to take advantage of this wonderful hue that is occurring now."

George glared at the young man and was about to speak when

something stopped him. His initial anger at being disturbed left him- as if their mere proximity soothed him. Their words seemed to affect him with a sense of naturalness. There was something about them that seemed almost calming.

"Well now," said George, his contempt tone usually reserved for tourists replaced with a pleasant air of friendliness, "So you folks are artists, huh."

"A type of artist," said the girl. She went on to explain that they were part of a group, a sort of loose partnership, that sought to help artists with certain mindsets capture things as they are. "In short," she said, "we are mixers."

George stared at the two incredulously.

"So you just travel around helping people mix paint?"

"Some people," replied the girl. "And we don't really help them mix. We offer a small amount of mixes we have; it is then for them to decide if it is right and then to match it if their desire is strong enough."

"I don't understand," George said, "Do you work for a paint company or something."

"Oh no, we don't work for anyone, and we're not selling anything," the girl responded reassuringly. "There is a lot of beauty in your world. It would be a shame to portray it on canvas unlike it really is. Don't you agree?"

"Well, sure, I guess I...," George stopped. "My world. You said my world," he stared at the young couple.

"There are many worlds, George," the man said, smiling.

How did he know my name, George was thinking.

But before he could respond, the man pointed to the steeple above the trees and said, "This is a difficult light you're trying to catch, considering the damp. Many would not even try." He pulled a small can from his case, opened it. "Would you care to try this mix to compare?"

George dipped his brush and stroked the paint across a section of the canvas.

"Oh my," he exclaimed. The color was perfect. He couldn't believe it. All this time and out of nowhere, there is the right mixture.

George glanced from the canvas, to the steeple and back again. It was as if the paint was the sun's rays and the rain combined. He was mesmerized by the result.

From behind him, he could hear the girl, barely audible, speaking. "We don't make much, so it you are pleased with that particular shade, it can serve as your model to match. Let your desire guide you."

As the realization of her comment hit him, he turned, speaking rapidly, "You mean you aren't going to leave me any to use!"

But the young couple was gone. And with them, the mixture. How could he ever match it? Well, he thought, it could be done; they did it. George felt a great rush of excitement at the prospect of the challenge. Now he did not need to wait for weather conditions to experiment because he had the color on this canvas. A matter of trial and error. May take a long time, but it could be done. I can do it, he thought, and then I can paint the scene true to life!

George looked again at the single brush stroke on the canvas. He knew down deep he might not be able to match that color. But he also knew he would try. He wanted to try. He drew a long sigh. "I am where I want to be, doing what I love and this will make it even more worthwhile." George realized he had spoken aloud and was even more surprised to hear the young woman's voice answer back.

"Here, take this. You are deserving," she said, holding the small metal container out to him.

Numbly, George accepted the container, knowing without opening it what it contained. With this he could find the exact color mix. He must get started. Oh, he quickly realized, I didn't thank her.

"Thank you so...," his voice trailed off when he realized she was gone again.

George stood quietly a moment longer, then smiling, turned to his paints and the beginning of his special creation. For some reason, it never occurred to him to wonder why the strange couple returned and left him the container; or for that matter why they appeared when they did. He was too busy with his brushes, oblivious to everything else-even the tourists who had gathered and were gawking over his shoulder, marveling at the realism his brush strokes were busy creating; his hand, it seemed, moving almost without thought, as if driven by some outside force, or perhaps guidance...

***

PEANUTS

I guess people probably see me as typical. Well, maybe not exactly typical, since by normal standards, I do tend to view some things a little differently than the run of the mill Joe.

I did the college thing; or at least for a short time. Didn't see much sense in it. Besides, it was boring to explain why I was majoring in philosophy, and my folks grew weary of the letters from school wanting to know when I planned to get serious about my education.

Still, I consider myself a reasonably normal young male. I like pretty girls, though I don't know many. My folks view me as a life-long bachelor, but that doesn't keep them from quizzing me occasionally about who I've met and what I'm gonna do with my life; you know, stuff like that. It doesn't help that I still live at home, though my folks' old rambling house, just off Cordova near the lake, is perfect for my endeavors. I pay a little rent, fix screen doors and such, so it works out OK. The occasional inquisition is worth the tradeoff, particularly the nearness of my lodging to downtown where I pick up a few bucks when I need it, sketching or doing tourist caricatures in the Plaza. Never even had a car. Don't need one.

Drawing is probably the only natural talent I have. Not sure why. My folks don't have any imagination at all. They're very normal. I had a few jobs, mainly to pacify their expectations, but none of 'em lasted very long. When I quit the last one, I received only a raised eyebrow from my parents; a good sign I think. Conveyed a sense of acceptance, or maybe resignation. My dad makes the occasional comment about the pittance I usually make sketching. He doesn't really hassle me though. I think he probably worries too much and is a little embarrassed when other people, particularly my uncle Jerry, make wisecracks.

Uncle Jerry is my Mom's brother and knows everything. Anyway, I guess what I earn doesn't seem like much to them, but I'm kinda quiet and laid back so I don't hustle the tourists as well as some in the Plaza. But, all in all, I get by.

I have a few friends. We meet for a beer or a movie every now and then, but usually I get bored pretty fast. I probably bore them as well because I don't talk too much. Never saw much need to; everyone else does enough. Don't really have a hobby other than sketching, though I have always hunted and fished. Never really shot anything, but the woods are nice. Most of the fish I catch, those times I actually bait my hook, usually get thrown back. Maybe that's part of the reason this really strange thing happened to me a few months ago. Check it out.

I was perched on my old fold up chair in the Plaza enjoying another one of those beautiful, sunny afternoons in St. Augustine. I had done one caricature and had five bucks to show for my day's work so far. As usual, in between turning tourists into exaggerated drawings, I was doing some Old Town scene sketching. I do lots of sketches. Anyway, I hear a voice just to my left rear.

"Rats, frigging hot dog."

I looked around. The nearest person was ole' John, hustling a tourist twenty feet away. That's strange, I thought, and turned back to my sketch board.

"Don't suppose you have any nuts, do you?"

I looked around again. Nothing.

"Hey dufus!"

Okay, someone's idea of a lame joke. I stood up and did a 360. Nobody there.

"How 'bout popcorn. Got any popcorn?"

My curiosity turning to anger, I searched again for the culprit, but the only other living thing near me was a squirrel, standing on hind legs peering at me with little beady eyes. In front of him were the remains of a discarded hot dog.

"How 'bout it. You got somethin' for me?"

The squirrel's mouth had moved and now he was staring at me expectantly.

"What the..."

"Hey lady, lady, how 'bout one of them peanuts."

"Oh, how cute", responded a strolling tourist eating a bag of peanuts. She threw the squirrel a nut.

"How 'bout a picture of you feeding me", the voice said.

"Well, that's unique, throwing your voice like that," the lady said, staring at me curiously.

"How much?"

Looking from the squirrel to the tourist and finally collecting myself, I answered, "With the squirrel in the picture too, I guess eight bucks."

"Okay."

The tourist's husband arrived just as I finished the picture. "Oh Tom," she said to him, "The cutest thing, this young man throws his voice like he's that squirrel talking." She looked at me. "Do it again."

Feeling suddenly helpless, I looked around. Nothing.

"I can't. My partner's gone," I said, glancing to the spot where the now absent squirrel had been perched.

"Oh, you're too cute," she laughed. Talking excitedly, picture in hand, she and Tom strolled away.

Well, I figured that was just about enough of this nonsense for the day. Besides, I did make a sale; or we made a sale, I thought, congratulating myself on such wit. Time to head home.

Needless to say, I had some strange dreams that night. As a matter of fact, I was convinced I had dreamed yesterday. Talking squirrels. The signal that it was time to get up came when Cheddar, my mother's cat, jumped into bed with me. It was a ritual. His day was usually ending when mine was beginning, so he took over the warm covers. I gave him a pat and said, "OK Cheddar, all yours".

The cat yawned and stretched, settling in.

"Looks like you can use it. Rough night, huh?"

Cheddar peered at me.

"Cat got your tongue?" I inquired.

No response.

"You know, I saw a squirrel yesterday that talked."

Cheddar came to a sitting position.

"Oh, so you're interested now huh? Maybe I should take you to the Plaza. Think you could drum up a customer for me?"

The cat cocked his head slightly, stretched again, and assumed his favorite position.

"Man, I gotta snap outa this. Well, at least you don't talk...do you?"

Cheddar closed his eyes and purred softly.

"OK, OK, I can take a hint." Leaving the cat to my room, I headed downstairs.

Uncle Jerry was in the kitchen pouring over the daily paper and sipping a late cup of coffee. When Uncle Jerry, a widower, retired, he moved in with us. He's an early riser and spends his day nosing into other people's business and talking. As I mentioned before, he knows everything. He goes to bed as the sun sets so he can be up early to keep up with everyone, and he's full of advice.

"Heard you talking to yourself upstairs," he said, when I sat down with my usual bowl of cereal. His ears are very large.

"I was talking to Cheddar."

"The cat?" he cackled. "He answer you back?"

"Did you hear him talking too?" I responded.

"Don't get all feisty," he said. "You wouldn't be so disagreeable if you got up earlier. You stay in bed too long." He eyed me with that all knowing look. "When you gonna settle down anyway. Ought to be somebody up there other than the cat for you to talk too. Ever think about that?"

"How can I not," I responded. "You remind me about twice a week. Besides, the cat sleeps more than I do, and lays out half the night. Why don't you go up and talk to him?"

"Well, I can't talk to you. I just think it's a shame, a grown man hanging out at that Plaza drawing, no real job and no desire to get on with his life."

"This is my life," I said. "I enjoy it. You ought to try it."

"I got things to do," he said in a huff. "Of course, nothing as important as your so called work day," he added sarcastically.

"It pays my bills," I said.

"I don't see how."

"Maybe I'll give myself a raise."

"Goodbye, Picasso," he said as he snatched up his cap and left the kitchen.

Well, I thought, watching him go, maybe that's why some think me strange; it's inherited.

Oh well, time for work.

The Plaza was bustling with activity when I finally arrived. John left his bead stand and walked over as I started setting up my stuff.

"Saw your little trick yesterday. Looks like it worked pretty good," he said.

"What trick?"

"You know, the squirrel thing; throwing your voice like that. Maybe you could teach one of 'em to draw." He laughed and strolled back to his stand where a customer was looking through beads.

Oh man, just what the world needs, another clown. I began working on the sketch I had started yesterday, quickly becoming engrossed in the task at hand.

"Not bad, but what about all those tourists passing you by? You're a real dufus!"

I looked up to see the squirrel staring at me. Well, whoever was pulling this prank was persistent. I looked around but other than tourists passing by and John stringing beads for someone, there was no one else there except me and the squirrel. I leaned over toward the squirrel, looking for wires or something to explain where the voice was coming from.

"Watch it, don't invade my space. You bring me something today?" The squirrel was on his hind legs peering at my bag on the ground.

"How 'bout a kick in the ass," I said sarcastically.

"Oh, that's great, I try to help you out yesterday and this is the thanks I get. And you can quit gawking at me like that; I'm not wired. See." The squirrel danced around in a small circle.

"So where's the voice coming from?"

"Where you think it's coming from? Geez, you're a real act, dufus. At least you could go over to St. George Street and get me some peanuts. I did get you a customer, which is more than you can say for yourself."

"What's that supposed to mean?"

"It means you sit here all day doing your little drawings while all these ripe tourists with money just pass you by. You got no salesman in you."

"And you could do better?" I still didn't believe this squirrel was talking, but somebody was.

"I already did. Yesterday. Tell you what, if I get you a customer in here in the next two minutes, will you get me some nuts?"

"You OK, man?" John had wandered over again and was giving me a quizzical look.

"Oh, oh sure, John, why?" I stammered.

"Well, you know, you seem to be jabbering away and there's no one here. Except your buddy there," he nodded toward the squirrel. "You better not carry your new gig too far, they might haul you away." He laughed and headed back to his stand.

"What's up with that dude," the squirrel was scratching his armpit.

"OK, that's it. I don't know who's doing this, but I'm not talking anymore. Some people think I'm strange enough as it is. The joke's over." I hurled a pencil at the squirrel.

Then, to my amazement, he put his hands on his hips-that's right, on his hips-and said, very defiantly, "OK, you need more convincing. Watch this."

The squirrel turned toward the sidewalk where tourists were strolling by. As two very macho looking men drew near, he turned to me and said "Watch this, target's at two o'clock."

In an animated voice, he said, "Hey, hey, is it true that you could tell your parents hated you as a kid because your bath toys were a toaster and electric radio?"

'Oh crap,' I'm thinking, 'I'm about to be killed'.

The two men stopped, looked at me, then at each other.

Before they could respond, the squirrel continued, "Yea, but you think you got problems, I was so ugly my father carried around a picture of the kid who came with his wallet."

One of the men now chuckling .

A good sign.

The squirrel is laughing at his own joke. "Hey, your buddy there said your girlfriend always wants to talk to you during sex, and just the other night she called you from a hotel."

Now both men are laughing.

The squirrel is howling.

"Man, you guys are so ugly, I heard you work in a pet shop and people keep asking you how big you'll get," the squirrel is definitely pushing his...my luck.

"He's gotta be talking about you, Joe," one of the men said to the other.

The furry varmint started up again, with great melodrama.

"You think you have problems; when I was born, the doctor came into the waiting room and said to my father, 'I'm sorry. We did everything we could, but he pulled through."

One of the men, over his laughter says, "Man, that's great. How do you throw your voice like that?"

Before I can respond, the other says, "Come on, Joe, let's get a picture of the two of us." Joe can't speak he's laughing so hard.

"How much for a picture? That's a great act," the same man says to me.

I glanced at the squirrel, who was holding both paws up, palms facing me with little fingers outstretched.

"Ten bucks," I said, double my normal price.

As the macho men were leaving with their picture, I turned back to the squirrel.

"Well," he said expectantly.

"OK, I'll go get nuts. Watch my stuff." What am I doing, I think, asking a squirrel to watch my stuff.

"John, would you watch my gear for a minute?" I said, regrouping.

"Sure, go ahead."

Off I went for nuts.

Well, the deal was struck. I gave the squirrel nuts, and he lured the customers in. He had an amazing knack for sizing up someone, then saying just the right thing to get their attention. Nearly all either bought a sketch or had a picture done. I was making more money than I ever had, and the squirrel was getting fat. But the topper to all this occurred at breakfast one Saturday morning a few weeks later.

My dad and I were having cereal. He's a live and let live kind of guy but is prone to worry on occasion. We were making small talk when he asked if I am keeping my eye out for a job, or was I interested yet in getting on with the city, where he worked. On cue, Uncle Jerry comes in and as usual, chimed in, "Yea, at least you'd make a little money and do something worthwhile."

"So I just need to make money and everyone would be happy," I responded.

"Well, no, that's not..." my dad started, but was interrupted by Uncle Jerry.

"Well, you sure don't make any hanging around that Plaza," he said.

I looked at my dad, who was focused on his cereal.

"I heard you have even started talking to yourself," Uncle Jerry continued.

My Dad looked up, seeming embarrassed.

"Oh, that's just some of my agent's advice," I said.

"Agent..." My dad started to speak, but again was cut off by the great philosopher, Jerry.

"Oh, so now you got an agent! Well, I'm sure that helps a lot," he said.

I reached into my baggy shorts and dropped a wad of bills on the table. "Oh, it helps a little."

They both stared at the money, dumbfounded.

"Well, I guess you are doing better than we thought," my dad said, looking at Uncle Jerry proudly. "But doesn't an agent cost a lot of money," he continued.

With my best secretive smile, I said, "No, Dad. This one's cheap. Works for peanuts."

***

54

JOKER

Joe arrived at the boat ramp as daylight was breaking. He quickly maneuvered the old Bronco II into position to launch his small boat. Backing down the ramp, he glanced around at the other vehicles parked in the large Trout Creek lot. As usual he thought, no Joker. Big surprise.

Joker was his best friend, though Joe frequently wondered why. They had grown up together, going through the usual boyhood adventures and now, at thirty-five years old, remained friends, though they had little in common beyond ballgames and fishing.

The only extended period of time Joe and Joker had been apart was the four years Joe had gone off to College. Joker had no interest in college, or much else for that matter, which turned out for the better since he barely made it through high school. Even doing that required Joe's help and urging.

As Joe finished launching the boat, without benefit of a guide due to Joker's tardiness, he parked the Bronco and headed back to the dock. Predictably, as he stepped into the boat, everything now ready to go, he heard Joker's old F-150 roaring down the tiny dirt road leading to the parking area. He arrived in a great cloud of dust, clamoring out of the truck before it rolled to a stop. Joe recalled the time Joker had done that at the local Dairy Queen and the truck rolled into the side of the ice cream parlor. But then, that was Joker. Joe was never sure whether Joker was just plain dumb, careless, or didn't care. Probably a little of each was usually his conclusion.

"Joey boy," Joker called out, trying to carry all his gear in one trip and dropping half of it on the way. "Whaz up?" Joker's beer belly was bouncing as he hurried toward the dock; as much as Joker could hurry.

"Joker, I thought we said 6:15," Joe called out, aggravated. It was now 6:45.

"Joey, I got up this morning, put a shirt on and a button fell off. Then I picked up my briefcase and the handle fell off. After that, I was afraid to go to the bathroom." Joker was chuckling at his own joke.

You now begin to sense how Joker came by his nickname.

"Joker, you don't even own a briefcase. Why can't you ever be on time?"

"Lighten up, Joey boy. We got all day. Besides, that was a great joke. You're way too serious."

"Do you need help with your stuff?" Dumb question. Joker always needed help.

"Nah, I got it," he replied, now retrieving a rod, towel, and bait bucket he had dropped along the way.

"You know what your problem is, Joey?" he asked, getting into the boat.

"Yea, putting up with your sorry ass," Joe replied.

"It goes back to when we were little, and remember when we played in the sandbox? You were so ugly the cat kept covering you up," his laughter echoing through the cypress trees around the docking area.

"Get in the fricking boat," Joe ordered.

"OK, OK," he responded, settling in.

Joe cranked the old motor and started to pull away when Joker suddenly yelled, "Wait, wait. I forgot the beer." Scrambling over rods and tackle, he ungracefully climbed onto the dock and headed back toward his pickup.

Well, thought Joe, my own fault. I saw he didn't have the perpetual beer cooler when he came down. Should have reminded him then. Joker's other major characteristic besides his good humor and playful manner was his unbelievable thirst for beer.

"Hurry up, man. Damn," said Joe, now truly aggravated.

"Now, now, Joey, you know you can't fish without beer. Wouldn't hardly be proper. Besides I just went to the doctor because I swallowed a bottle of sleeping pills, and he told me to have a few drinks and get some rest," he waited like a small child to make sure Joe got the joke. When no laughter was forthcoming, he said, "Don't you get it, Joey, the doctor...." Joe cut him off, snapping, "Joker, get your cooler and get in the boat."

"Joey," he said, returning with cooler in hand, "I swear, you're just no fun at all since you got married," referring to the wedding this past year, for which of course, Joker was the best man.

"Well, maybe you should try it. Might make you a little easier to be around, and you could definitely use help keeping yourself organized."

"You must be crazy! Having to get permission to go to the pool hall or watch a ballgame. Not me, man."

"Probably just as well, because I can't think of a woman that would have your sorry ass anyway," Joe responded, a little more playfully.

Predictably, his comment reminded Joker of yet another joke.

"Not true, Joey. Just yesterday a gal called me up and said 'come on over, nobody's home.' So I went over. Nobody was home."

Joe stared at his friend for a moment. "I heard that one before. Just like I have heard most of your jokes."

Joker began fumbling around in the cooler for a beer.

"Joker, it isn't even 7:30. How can you drink a beer?" Dumb question. Joker could always drink beer.

Getting no response, Joe asked, "Want to try the Shands? See if we can pick a red up," referring to the two mile long bridge that connected the west bank of the St. John's River at Green Cove Springs to the east bank at Orangedale.

"Nah, let's go over to the cove," referring to Coley Cove.

"I don't know. All those pilings. I'm always afraid I'll get the boat hung up on one. Besides, we lose a hundred hooks fishing around those things."

"Ah, come on. It's the lucky place today. This old boat ain't worth anything anyhow," Joker urged.

That was probably true. The old wooden boat had seen better days, but Joe loved it, which was why he was always leery about getting on stumps or old pilings. The bottom was not the soundest in the world.

"Alright," he said, "but we'll anchor off the pilings. I don't want to get right on top of them."

"OK, skipper, whatever you say," replied Joker with his 'I knew I'd talk you into it' grin.

They headed toward the cove, enjoying the crisp fall morning.

About halfway there, Joker began taking his shoes off. Not an unusual phenomenon, even in cool weather. Joe never understood why he enjoyed being barefoot so much; unless, of course, he was planning on doing some counting and needed his toes. He recalled the time they had been pulled over by a traffic cop for a minor infraction. The cop, noting that Joker was barefoot, pointed out that it was illegal to drive barefoot. Joker had responded that because his foot was so large, size 14, it was safer for him to drive this way because his large shoes kept getting hung under the pedals. The cop just shook his head and let them go without a citation. That was Joker. Always finding the humor in any situation. Sometimes it was contagious. Sometimes monotonous.

"Hey Joe, did I tell you about the blonde that showed up at the emergency room with her index finger gone?"

"No, and I don't suppose it would do any good to tell you I don't care," Joe responded.

Undeterred, Joker continued, "Yea, her finger's gone so the doc says 'what happened to your finger?' So the blond says, 'Well, I decided to commit suicide so I put a pistol to my chest, but then I remembered my boob job and didn't want to mess that up. So then I decided to take sleeping pills, but they make you so sleepy.' Now the doc says, 'But what about your finger?' Well, says the blond, I decided to put the pistol in my ear, you know, so it wouldn't mess my face up. But then I remembered how much noise a gun makes, so I stuck this finger in the other ear for the noise and blew it right off."

Joker was howling.

"Joker, do me a favor. Don't tell any more jokes until we get where we're going," Joe asked calmly.

"OK, Joey boy. I need another beer anyway."

"So how's the crabbing?" Joe asked, referring to Joker's primary occupation, though not his only one.

"Kinda slow right now. Might have to call the old man and do a little construction stuff."

Joker's father was a successful building contractor. The disappointment of his life had been Joker's total disinterest in the business, though he worked as a hired hand on occasion when his crabbing or other such endeavors were slow.

"Why don't you quit that nonsense and go in with your dad like he's always wanted?"

"Nah, I get no respect from the old man. Why, when I was growing up I asked him how to get my kite in the air, and he told me to run off a cliff."

"I'm serious, Joker. We're not getting any younger you know and we're not little boys anymore. Don't you want to do something you can make a living at, something you'd like to do."

"I am making a living and I'm doing what I like to do."

"Well, you know we can't always do exactly what we want to. Sometimes to get ahead, you have to do other things."

"No," replied Joker, a little more seriously, "I don't know that. Don't you think people ought to do what they want to if they can?"

"Well, yes, to the extent they can. But you need to think about the future. You can't crab and bounce around from job to job your whole life."

"Now see, Joey boy. That's where we have always been different. You're always so serious. How are you any happier than I am. I love my life, and I like breaking the monotony of doing the same old thing day in and day out. Where's the fun in that?"

"No one said it was supposed to be fun, Joker. You have to make a living and prepare for old age."

"Well that's just plain stupid. You mean I shouldn't do what I want to now so I can make more money and be good to go in old age? That's stupid. Besides, I was so poor growing up, if I hadn't been a boy I wouldn't have had anything to play with," his joke signifying the end of the serious conversation. Serious was one thing Joker never seemed to like.

They entered the cove and Joe approached the piling area cautiously. At one time there had been several docks here, long ago rotted away. The pilings, most under the surface of the water, were all that was left. Fishing was usually good but the pilings could be a real pain trying to work around. Fish had to be brought in quickly and carefully before they became wrapped around one of the old posts.

Joe broke out his surprise of the day. A new baitcaster reel he was dying to try.

"Whoa, that's a beauty, Joey boy. When did you get that?"

"Just got it this week. Haven't had a chance to try it out yet." Joe began rigging his new toy.

"Well, it ain't gonna help you out fish me. Let me show you how it's done." Joker started flipping his old spinning reel toward the pilings. He immediately caught a nice shellcracker.

"Yo, hoss. Come on now. Get in this boat with your daddy." Joker couldn't fish without talking. Matter of fact, Joker couldn't do anything without talking.

"Hey Joe, did I tell you my airline jokes?" Before Joe could answer, Joker began, "The pilot comes on the loudspeaker and says, 'We are pleased to have some of the best flight attendants in the industry...sadly, none of them are on this flight'." Chuckling, he continued, "Later, after a bumpy landing, one of the attendants comes on the speaker and says, 'We ask you to please remain seated while Captain Kangaroo bounces us to the terminal'."

Shaking his head, Joe finished rigging his reel and cast between two pilings.

Almost immediately he got a strike, set the hook, and the pole bent double. "Oh yeah," he exclaimed. But the fish ran around a piling and the line became taut, hung on the pole.

"Give it slack, man. Work it to the left there." Joker started giving his sage advice.

"Joker, just fish and let me work this." Joe snapped.

"OK, man, but I'm telling you, you're gonna break your line if you keep tugging like that."

The line snapped.

"Damn." Joe said disgustedly.

"Told you, man. You gotta finesse it." He jerked his rod. Another fish on. "Hey now. Come on big boy." He worked the fish to the boat and lifted it over. "Come on, Joey boy." Joe was busy re-rigging his new reel.

Joker dropped the fish into the livewell and popped another beer top. "So, Joey, this guy gets on an airplane and sits down by this gorgeous blonde. They take off and he notices she is leafing through some papers. He peeks and sees the word sex several times, and pictures of sexual things. 'That looks interesting', he says to her. 'Oh', she says, 'I lecture on sex related things.' 'Are you a therapist?' he asks. 'No, it's more of a cultural thing. Myths about sexual activity.' 'What do you mean?' he asks. 'Well, like the common belief that black men are the most well endowed males when actually the American Indian male seems to actually hold that distinction. Although Jewish men seem to make the best lovers, the best all around male sexual type, you know size, technique, and so on is, believe it or not, the southern redneck.' She looks at the guy and says, 'Oh, I'm sorry, I didn't introduce myself. I'm Alice Daniels.' The man looks at her and says, 'Hi, Alice, my name is Tonto Goldstein, but my friends call me Bubba."

"Very funny." Joe said over Joker's howling.

Joker finally collected himself and said, "Let's move in closer, Joey, so we can work around these pilings."

"I don't know, Joker. I don't want to get the boat on those things. My whole bottom is fiberglass patch now."

"Come on, man, ease her up. Let's get at these fish."

" Let's do it, Joey," Joker continued when Joe did not respond.

Man, how many times have we been through this scene, Joe was thinking. Joker urging some action, usually resulting in a catastrophe. Still, it would be good to get a little closer. As usual, he relinquished.

"Alright, get the anchor, but we gotta be careful." Joe started easing the boat forward. Suddenly, it stopped. He put the motor in reverse, but the boat just rocked. "Damit, Joker, I told you this was a bad idea." The boat was grounded on a piling. He put the boat in forward again and eased the throttle forward. Bad idea. The tip of the piling came through in the center of the bow. "Oh shit. Move to the back," he yelled at Joker, who was already moving his large frame to the rear. Joe joined him there and together they rocked the boat. It came loose, but water was gushing in through the hole.

"Damn, what are we gonna do now?" Joe thought of his new reel and all their tackle. They could swim the half mile to shore, but everything else would be lost. When will I learn, he thought.

"Hang on, Joey boy. No sweat." Grabbing a can of beer, he forced it into the hole. Nice tight fit. He then jerked his shirt off and stuffed it around the can into the small openings left. The rush of water subsided, but the boat was flooded.

Grabbing the bait bucket, Joker yelled, "Plane'er up Joey."

Joe hit the throttle while Joker started bailing with the bucket. Soon, he had enough water out and the boat slowly planed up, the bow lifting and the hole rising above the water line.

"Home free, Joey boy. Guess we're done fishing though."

Joe, feeling some relief that at least they should get back OK and save their gear, wasn't sure whether he was pissed or happy to get out of the situation. Neither spoke on the trip back.

They finally reached the boat ramp and silently began loading the boat onto the trailer. When that was done, Joe inspected the hole, with Joker's beer can still in place.

"Why don't you take those fish I caught," Joker said, as if hoping that would help the situation.

Receiving no answer, he began transferring his gear to the old pickup. When that was completed, he pulled the beer can from the hole and popped the top. He shifted from foot to foot, glancing at Joe out of the corner of his eye, as if making eye contact might worsen things.

Joe still had not spoken.

"Well, I guess I'll go then," said Joker, turning toward his truck, head down.

Joe watched his big friend go. They had played this scene many times in their lives. Joker was always creating mischief, or screwing up in some lame attempt at a practical joke. But he was also the one who came at two A.M. to pick you up when your car broke, or showed up to help repair the roof. It was with Joker in mind that the love-hate phenomenon was created.

Joker glanced back as he was fumbling for his car key, as if looking for some sign, but Joe, securing his gear, worked silently.

Joker cranked his old truck.

"Joker." Joe walked toward the truck. "You know, I heard when you were born, the doctor came into the waiting room and said to your father, 'I'm sorry. We did everything we could, but he pulled through anyway." A smile began to play around his lips. "Come on big guy. Follow me home and we'll get some chow and have a look at the hole."

"Now you talking, Joey boy," Joker said, breaking into a big grin. "Say, did I tell you the one about....."

***

MIKE'S BIRDS

The shoreline in this area of Florida was very rocky, rough to traverse by foot. Few people ever ventured here because there really was no beach, certainly not compared to most of coastal Florida. This suited Mike Arness fine. He enjoyed the solitude. Fishing was not that great either, and that made it all the more private. Most boats he encountered turned out to be drunken pleasure boaters, to whom he was more than happy to give directions to better fishing areas miles away.

Although the area was not easily accessible by road, a few tourists ventured through but unimpressed by the rough beach, and difficulty getting to it, left quickly. Mike was one of a very few full time residents out here. Most houses, like his, were very small and used for occasional retreats. The run down cottage he rented was owned by New York yankees, whom he had seen only one time in the two years he had been their tenant; to Mike, this was a perfect situation.

Mike had found this place quite by accident right after his release from Army service. Life here quickly became a comfortable routine. He discovered that the rocky beach held many treasures in the form of shells, unique stones, glass worn perfectly smooth by sand and water interaction, and other items brought to shore by the incoming tide. He had developed several gift shop contacts in St. Augustine who bought his treasures and turned them into tourist novelties. This endeavor, coupled with occasional work repairing electronic gadgets for a small shop in town, using his Army training, met his financial needs most of the time; there were times, however, when he ate a lot of fish and crabs. Mike was very content with his quiet way of life; he particularly liked being his own boss. About a year ago, that life changed abruptly.

The day started innocently enough. He was on the beach early, lugging his small inflatable on his back. The plan was to wait for the fog to lift and get in some fishing before the swells got too rough. He pumped up the inflatable and sat patiently on his favorite large rock, gazing through the lifting fog at the distant ocean. When the low horizon looked clear enough, he picked up his binoculars, hoping to spot fish activity in the distance. What he saw instead was several dorsal fins just beyond the gentle breakers. At first, he assumed it was a school of sharks, and then on closer scrutiny, recognized the gently curling fins and graceful leaps.

"Dolphins," he spoke aloud.

Dropping the binoculars, he dashed back up the high sand dunes to his old truck, where he snatched up his mask and snorkel, running and stumbling back to the inflatable. He rowed into the swells until the water was deep enough for his tiny engine. As he moved slowly out, top speed for the small Merc, he could now clearly see the pranksters playing gleefully in the calm water. As he watched them play, Mike was carried back to his childhood and the start of his love affair with these happy-go-lucky creatures.

The summer of his twelfth birthday, his family had vacationed in Florida. Mike and many other children had quickly discovered the schools of spotted dolphins that came to play daily in the shallows. To their delight, the children realized some dolphins seemed to enjoy giving them rides. Mike's initial hesitation about trusting these animated beasts instantly disappeared with the exhilaration of being hauled through the water at amazing speeds and joining the dolphins at play.

He spent all his vacation days that summer swimming with the dolphins. Frequently, they would carry him several hundred feet off shore where it was still not exceptionally deep, and he would marvel at the marine activity on the ocean floor. On one such trip, he was hanging onto his gleeful host watching a school of fish below when he saw a long shadow moving under him, followed by the huge shark that cast it.

Mike became terrified. Suddenly, as if sensing his fear, the dolphins around him began making clicking noises. The shark turned, saw the dolphins, and sped away. The dolphins, obviously happy with their performance, turned and towed Mike closer to shore. It was a summer he would never forget.

Now, 15 years later, he still loved these animals and could not resist the opportunity to join them. In truth, he had come to admire and respect all wildlife. After his release from the Army, the abundance of wildlife, including the ocean and its creatures, caused him to settle here.

As Mike arrived among the dolphins he donned his mask and snorkel and slipped over the side of the boat. Predictably, the dolphins immediately surrounded him, ready for play. He became so engrossed in his dolphin activity, he had not noticed a sport fishing boat approaching. When he heard voices, he turned and saw the boat with three men in it. Obviously fisherman. One of the men had a large fish hooked and was shouting instructions to another man piloting the boat; a third was sipping beer, observing the fight.

Some of the curious dolphins moved toward the boat. Suddenly, one of the men yelled, "Shark." His fish, a large king mackerel, broke the water and the shark was looking for supper.

The pilot began cursing and grabbed a small caliber rifle from the console. He began shooting at the shark and to his horror; Mike saw that some of the dolphins had surrounded the shark, in the line of fire. Mike yelled and swam toward the boat. One of the dolphins made a high squealing noise.

"Stop," Mike yelled, now along side the boat, "You're hitting the dolphins."

"What the hell," the fisherman said, "Mind your own business, I ain't losing this fish."

Mike swam for the fish, now only about ten feet from the boat. He grabbed his diving knife and cut the line. The fish dove, with the shark in pursuit.

"You son of a bitch," said the fisherman as he dropped his rod and grabbed an oar, trying to hit Mike over the side of the boat.

"Don, help me get this asshole," he yelled at the third man, who was still calmly looking on. Don just smiled, taking it all in, but continued sipping his beer.

Mike turned and headed back to his inflatable. As he passed the rear of the sport boat, he reached up and tore the gas line from the outboard. It was very satisfying but unfortunately another boat had arrived on the scene. It was a wildlife officer.

"That son of a bitch cut my fishing line and broke my motor," yelled the fisherman, "I want to press charges."

Two weeks later, Mike arrived at the St. Johns County Courthouse in response to the summons he had received. His case was called and the judge peered down at him. "Are the complainants present?" the judge inquired. The three men from the boat stood up. "Tell me what happened," said the judge. Two of the men voiced their complaint. The third, Don, stood by silently.
When they were through speaking, the judge glanced at Mike, "All that true, son?"
"Yea, I guess it is, your honor," replied Mike.
"Well, young man, I see from the file here that other than shell collecting, you don't seem to be employed. What do you do when you're not cutting fishing lines and destroying private property?" The judge waited for his answer.
"Sir, I was trained as a microwave technician in the Army, and I work part time in a small electronic repair shop," Mike said.
"How much do you work there?" the judge wanted to know.
"Well, not a lot. Enough to pick up a few bucks." Mike began to feel uneasy.
"Maybe if you had a job, you wouldn't get into trouble," the judge said. "But since you don't, why shouldn't I put you to work out at the county farm?"
Before Mike could reply, the man named Don spoke for the first time, "Your honor, may I approach?"
"Sure, come on up."
Don went forward and stopped beside Mike. "Can you work on microwave relays and transmitters?" he asked Mike.
"Well, yes I can."
Don turned to the judge and said, "Your honor, I'll give him a job."
The judge, taken aback, thought for a moment, then said to Mike, "Tell you what, son, if you accept this gentleman's job and pay for the boat repair, I'll just put you on probation. That OK with you?"
The prospect of having a boss again did not appeal to Mike; but

neither did the alternative.

"Well, son," said the judge, waiting for an answer.

"Yes sir, I agree"

"Very well. This case is finished. You go with your new boss and don't let me see you in here again." He rapped his gavel sharply. Don turned and said, "Come with me." Mike followed him outside.

Don turned to him on the courthouse steps, "Mike is it?" he asked.

"That's right," replied Mike.

"OK, let's get something straight," Don started, "Don't think I'm your sugar daddy. I didn't bail your ass out in there because I'm a crusader. I think you're probably a wiseass punk, too lazy to work. My reasons for this are simple. I'm the field boss for a cellular phone outfit. My division maintains and repairs our relay sites, mostly microwave dishes. You told the judge you have military training in that area, and you're obviously a beach bum that likes to be left alone, so here's the deal."

He stared at Mike and continued, "I have several sites along the shoreline: some on shore, some one or two miles off shore. It costs me time and money to keep them up. When I send my techs out to do the job, they piss away days getting boats and equipment together. Then half the time they either get lost or spend my money fishing, while other jobs get behind. If you get through our refresher training, I'll pay you a part time salary, no benefits, to keep the sites up out in your area. You use your own boat, and I'll provide tools and a cellular phone, which we'll use to coordinate jobs. You come to the office every two weeks or so to do paperwork; otherwise, you're still on your own. Work on your own time as long as the job gets done. You can still be a bum and pick up a few bucks, and stay out of jail, of course."

He paused, then continued, "Well what about it? Deal, or does the work farm appeal to you more?"

Mike pondered the offer, "Can I get a new boat motor?"

"No," replied Don. "We'll pay to keep yours up, within reason."

"OK," said Mike, "I'll do it."

"Well, that's real big of you. A couple of other things... are you one of those candy ass environmentalists, because this is not a back to nature club."

"No," replied Mike, "I just don't hold with idiots harming defenseless creatures."

"Well, that's good," said Don, "Because this isn't a save the whale organization. We have a job to do and we do it, understand?"

"Yes, I understand," replied Mike.

"OK, the other thing is I have to sell this to my boss, John Allen. He's a hard ass, probably won't like you at all. But he usually lets me do my own hiring. He's just picky because we have had some real worthless types come through."

He handed Mike a card. "Come to the office tomorrow at eight o'clock sharp and I'll introduce you to John. If he agrees, we'll do the paperwork and get you in training. Questions?"

"No," replied Mike, "I'll be there."

The next day Mike showed up and met John. He was not happy with the situation and made no secret about it, but because of his obvious respect for his field boss, he grudgingly agreed to the plan. "Let's get him trained and see what he's got. If he screws up or wastes our time, he's gone." warned John.

That was a year ago and things had gone pretty well. Mike still had plenty of time to enjoy the ocean, even when working, and the extra cash was nice. He had even picked up a new, bigger inflatable, which allowed him to go further out on dives. Don rode Mike's ass hard, and he came to hate his infrequent trips to the office where John always had plenty of beach bum comments. Don was a fair man but didn't like to hear excuses for not getting jobs done. He was a serious company man, but easier to take than John who, Mike was convinced, would fire him at the least provocation. Anyway, he didn't have to see either one of them that often, except for the occasional 'surprise' visits by Don when a job had not been reported done. All in all though it was a good situation.

Today, Mike was on his way off shore in his new inflatable. One of the larger microwave relay sites, H4, needed a new cone and re-orienting. It would take the better part of a day, but with luck, he might get in an hour of dive time afterwards. As he approached the H4 site, about two miles out, he could see the high H-pattern stand taking shape, rising about twenty feet above the ocean surface. Now he could see the back-to-back relay dishes, their large cones jutting outwards, and something else.

Something was on top of, and between the two cones. A pelican maybe, he thought. As he approached one of the large pilings to tie up, he could see it was not a pelican. It appeared to be a stack of debris of some kind. Oh well, he thought, I'll have to clean that out of the way before I can orient the dishes.

Strapping on his tool belt and safety harness, he began the climb up. As he neared the top to grab the timber for the shimmy over to the cones, he saw movement. Oh shit, he thought, what do we have here? The answer became obvious when a huge osprey stuck its head out.

The large bird gave a shrill cry and spread its large wings, about five feet across. He stared at Mike with piercing yellow eyes, then rose up and soared away.

"Well, at least he didn't attack me," Mike whispered to himself.

He shimmied over to the dish to have a closer look at the nest, thinking it was a shame he had to tear it down, but there was no way he could re-orient the large discs without doing so. He could probably replace the cones, but without the follow-on disc adjustments, the signal could be irregular, which would not make all the cell phone users very happy, and certainly not Don, or butt hole John.

He was now next to the large nest. He studied the impressive structure: branches, some as big as an inch around, blended with chunks of moss and other vegetation. It was about eighteen inches across and perhaps two feet high. Mike was impressed at how many trips it must have taken the osprey to get all this stuff out here, almost two miles from shore. He planned his next move, thinking he might be able to just move the nest, but it quickly became obvious he would have no way to anchor it. The osprey had actually managed to jam it between the cones in such a way that not even a strong wind would destroy it.

"Well," he thought, "No need to procrastinate."

He got his balance and undid the safety harness. As he rose to re-clip it to the riser pole above him, he could now see into the nest.

"Oh no," he spoke aloud. In the bottom of the nest were three large eggs. Mike sat back down on the beam. "Well, this changes things," he thought.

Mike sat trying to figure out what to do. He knew there was no way he could now destroy the nest. His head filled with questions: how long before they hatch and fly away? How long could he put off the cone work? Don was already on his case because the signal intermittently faded. He had four other routine maintenance jobs to do over the next few days, so he decided to postpone the dilemma here, risking the wrath of Don, as well as John. He left the stand and headed back to shore to get one of the other jobs done.

The next day, still pondering the nest crisis, Mike decided to take his shells into town to pick up a few extra bucks. He lucked out and found a parking space by the plaza and headed for his favorite gift shop customer. The shop owner, George, was alone when he entered.

"Hey, Mike," George greeted him, "How's it going?"

"Good, George, how about you?"

"Oh, can't complain. Kinda slow though. What you got for me?"

"Some pretty good ones today, have a look," Mike handed him the bag.

As George went over to a table to lay the shells out, Mike wandered around the store. It always amazed him to see the variety of trinkets that George and others made using seashells. He walked over to where several ceramic looking birds and sea animals were displayed. Picking up one, he said, "This is nice."

George glanced up from the shells. "Oh yea," he said, "An osprey. That's a good likeness, but nothing like the real McCoy. They're really neat birds."

"How so?" asked Mike.

"Well, they're kinda like eagles, great hunters, very strong talons, and they usually have only one mate. Very independent too. No feeding crumbs to those guys, like stupid pigeons and gulls; these fellows do their own thing, very proud bird." George continued sorting through the shells.

"How many eggs do they lay?" asked Mike.

"Oh, it varies, two or three. Sometimes more. Choose their nest site very carefully and take turns hauling in stuff to build it. Then they seem to watch it for a while; like making sure everything is OK before nesting. But I'm not an expert."

He looked at Mike. "Why so much interest?"

"Just curious," replied Mike. "How long to hatch?"

"Several weeks I guess, don't know for sure." George went on, "They seem to be good parents. Very protective."

George turned back to the shells. "Give you fourteen bucks for the lot," he said.

"How much for this?" Mike asked, still holding the ceramic bird.

Surprised, because Mike had never purchased any of his gifts, George said, "Oh, that's thirty-two bucks, plus tax. Nice piece though."

Mike grimaced. George understood the look.

"Tell you what," he said, "Take the bird for these shells and your next delivery," he paused, "But do me a good job on the next load."

"Deal," Mike said, "See you in a couple of weeks."

Walking to his truck, Mike reviewed the situation. There was no way to know when the eggs were laid; it could be several weeks before the nest was clear. On the other hand, if they were ready to hatch, it might only be several days. But he really couldn't wait that long, and he knew there was no need to explain this to Don. His job was to keep the cellular traffic clear and customers happy. No way he would put off the maintenance, particularly since there was already intermittent signal trouble. Mike glanced at the bird he had placed on the seat of his truck. "You could cost me my job," he said to the ceramic statute. The decision made, he began planning how to buy some time.

Three days passed, and now the ringing cell phone showed Don's number on the caller ID. Mike took a deep breath and answered, talking rapidly, "Don, I was gonna call you," he said, "I need to come in for more parts for two of the shore sites. They're borderline, but I thought I'd go ahead and do replacements, as well as paint the brackets while the weather is good." He waited.

"That's fine," Don said. "How 'bout the other sites?" he asked.

"Oh, they're fine, just routine stuff," then added, "Except maybe the relay house at Vilano might need some relay replacement." He waited.

"What about H4?" Don asked.

Mike thought quickly. "It's not that bad. Thought I'd do this other stuff first." He held his breath.

"Well," replied Don, "Be a good time to go out, while the weather's calm."

"Probably so. I'll try to fit it in over the next few days," Mike said and then paused.

"Alright, give me your parts list."

Relieved, Mike read off the things he needed, feeling somewhat guilty since some were not needed at all.

The next day Mike called Don and explained that he had truck trouble. He would be in the next day. Don was not happy, but seemed to accept his white lie. Another day bought. When he did finally pick his parts up the next day, Don quizzed him suspiciously about his sites. Mike assured him that everything was under control, to which Don said, "Fine. Just stay on schedule and don't start screwing around; and don't forget about H4. It'll start getting stormy soon."

"No problem," replied Mike, "I'm on it."

He left the office and decided on the way back to check the nest. The inflatable was in the back of his truck, and it was too late to get anything else done. Maybe he could find a few shells on the beach, as well.

Mike approached the H4 site slowly. The osprey peered over the side of the nest, but did not fly away. He took his binoculars out and watched the bird, who stared back defiantly. Mike lowered the binoculars and cranked his engine. Maybe she's nesting, he thought. Even so, how long before they hatched and left. What a mess. He thought again about just telling Don what was going on, but quickly abandoned that idea knowing he would just tell him to do the job. Besides, if the signal deteriorated any more, John would get complaints and that would be that. He had reached the shore and decided to forget his bird problem for a while and collect some shells.

Another week passed and the only thing he heard from Don was a cell message giving him new coordinates for orienting one of the shore sites. He did that and called the office after hours to avoid talking to Don to report the job done. He also left a message saying he needed new clamps and braces for a shore site several miles south, and that he would pick them up in a few days. He added that he might stay down at that site a day or two to look around. Might as well buy some more time, he thought. But his anxiety about this charade was growing.

Mike was now enroute to the office for his parts, some of which were bogus. This caused him a little guilt, but he justified it by telling himself that they would eventually have to be replaced anyway. He timed his arrival with a time he knew Don would almost surely be at lunch, to avoid an inquisition. He knew his parts would be in a box with his name on it, so he could get in and out quickly.

As he had planned, Don was not there. Unfortunately, John was.

"Mike," he yelled from his office.

"Yessir," responded Mike.

"Come in here a minute," John said. "Have you talked to Don?"

"Not for a couple of days, why?" Mike asked.

"We're still getting a signal drop at H4 so you may have screwed up the re-orientation or cone adjustment."

Mike hesitated, deciding whether to say he had not gotten to the job yet, saving his professional pride; his jobs were always right. Instead, he just said, "OK, I'll check it." Oh, man, he thought, now I'm lying and misleading, all over stupid birds. He left the office quickly.

Several days passed and Mike was once again on his way to H-4. He arrived to a quiet scene. No movement from the nest. He gathered his harness and climbed the stand. No sign of the osprey. He reached the beam, quickly hooked off and peered into the nest. Three baby ospreys chirped with wide-open mouths at the anticipation of food. A high shrieking from behind him announced the arrival of mama osprey, who obviously was not happy with the intruder. Mike scrambled down the stand to his boat as the huge bird landed on the nest, staring at him intently. Her large wings were extended, as if ready to attack at any moment. What a magnificent creature, Mike thought. "I'd better get the hell outta here before I'm bombed," he spoke aloud.

Mike's mind raced as he headed back to shore. The good news was the eggs had finally hatched. The bad news, not long ago. The chicks were very small. Realistically, Mike appraised, he would never get away with this caper; the chicks would be lost and he'd certainly get fired in the process.

Sure enough, three days later, Don called and demanded to know what was up with H4.

"What do you mean?" Mike asked innocently.

"I mean," Don shouted, "The signal drop is worse, and John just chewed my ass out. He said he told you to square it away over a week ago."

"OK, OK," Mike said. "I've just been busy with all the other stuff, I'll check it out."

"Half of that 'other stuff'," Don responded sarcastically, "Could have waited. Get off your ass and get with it." He hung up.

Mike was in very deep now. One way or the other, he would probably lose his job, but he had decided he must protect the nest, so there was no way he could work on the dish. The problem now was how to keep someone else from working on it, in case Don really got impatient or even fired him. He needed more time and could only think of one way to get it.

The first part of his plan required figuring out a way to get some signal change to the plus side out of H4. This would at least cause Don to think he was working on the problem. He was searching his mind for solutions, recalling those times in the military when parts were in short supply, or not accessible in the field, when 'field expediency' procedures had to be employed. This simply meant 'jerry-rigging' to get the most out of what you had. He started going through the used parts he had replaced as well as new ones destined for other jobs. Suddenly, it hit him.

If he could rig a smaller dish and cone below the double primary dish and tie it all together, it might provide enough boost to increase signal power. He knew it would definitely not be the same as total replacement, but it could be enough to hold down complaints and keep Don's attention off H4. He had many other problems. But could he erect the extra dish by himself quickly enough so the osprey would not get upset and abandon the nest? George said they were good parents, but how much intrusion would they tolerate before survival instinct took over? He had to try something, and this seemed to be the only course of action available.

The temporary fix identified, part two of the plan was to install this smaller dish quickly to avoid involving Dave, the senior tech that Don, if he ran out of patience, would surely send to H4. Dave had evolved into the unofficial troubleshooter for the company. He was very knowledgeable and during Mike's training last year Dave had been his teacher. They had immediately hit it off and occasionally met for breakfast. In truth, Dave had taken Mike under his wing. For that very reason, Mike did not want to put his friend in an awkward situation that could cost Dave his job.

The part of the plan which required Dave's help would have to be handled very carefully without him knowing the real reason. Mike began gathering the needed parts he had on hand, at the same time planning his phone call the next day, after his trip to H4.

The next morning he loaded his gear into the inflatable and headed out to sea. A quarter mile from H4, he cut the engine and picked up his binoculars. Mama osprey was perched atop the nest gazing around. After several minutes, she took off toward the coast. Mike timed the absence. Forty minutes later she returned with something in her mouth and began feeding the chicks. When that task was completed, she went back to her guard duty. Two hours later Mike was beginning to wonder if she would ever leave again.   Then suddenly, she took off. Mike cranked the motor, his mind racing. He had about forty minutes to get there, pull the dish in place and drill the holes. There would not be time for mounting and connecting everything. "Come on, motor, faster," he said aloud.

Mike was tying the boat before it ever stopped. He grabbed the pulley, its end rope already connected to the dish. Ignoring the safety harness, he scrambled up the piling, the pulley hook in one hand. He quickly slipped the hook into the existing eyebolt, put there for that purpose. Working with his arms wrapped around the piling, he pulled the heavy dish up and tied it off, still dangling. Grabbing the cordless drill he drilled the two mounting bracket holes and checked the time. Fifteen minutes left, assuming the osprey stayed on schedule. He could hear the chicks above his head. Resisting the temptation to take a look, he decided to go ahead and bolt the brackets in place. With the last bolt in place, he heard the unmistakable shriek of mama returning. He quickly lashed the dangling dish to the pole and practically slid down its rough surface to the boat landing in a not so graceful heap on one of the hard wooden slats.

Leaving the osprey with wings spread and angry sounds spilling from her beak, he fired the engine and soared off. "Damn birds," he said, " Don't appreciate anything."

He decided it would be better to forget the final mounting and hookup today, since he was unsure how much intrusion mama would take before flying the coop. He pulled up to the shore and reached for his cell phone.

Don answered with a gruff hello. It had been one of those days.

"What is it?" Don asked without enthusiasm.

Mike continued, "The back-up Ponte Vera site has been vandalized. I need you to send Dave down tomorrow with these parts." He read them off.

"Dammit, Mike, why do you need Dave? Who did it, any idea?"

"I don't know who did it, and I need Dave because we'll have to feed new wire up," Mike gave his rehearsed answer. He held his breath, hoping Don wouldn't send someone else, or worse yet, come himself. He could picture Don flipping through job sheets and checking parts inventory.

Finally, he responded, "OK, I'll send Dave. Do you need him to help you with H4 too, since you obviously haven't done it."

"No, no, I was about to do it when this came up. It's next up."

"It better be," Don said gruffly.

Mike put the phone away with a sigh of relief. He felt somewhat guilty about the deception and the extra work he was causing, but it would only involve Dave's time; he would keep the parts he was on his way to 'vandalize' for use on other jobs later, so at least there would be no monetary loss to the company.

Several hours later, with the removed parts rattling around in the back of his truck, he headed home. On impulse, he stopped at the St. Johns County Library to get more information about these stupid birds he was trying to help. To his dismay, the library was closing. He hadn't realized it was so late. Oh well, he thought , be nice to know more about the probable cause of me getting fired. "Damn things will probably turn out to be a sea buzzards anyway," he said aloud.

Dave was waiting for Mike when he arrived at the 'vandalized' site the next morning. He was surveying the missing equipment.

"Interesting vandals," Dave said, "looks like they neatly removed the equipment." He eyeballed Mike.

"Hey, Dave, how you been. Yea, looks like they wanted some parts. Didn't really seem to damage or deface anything." Mike was a little nervous.

Dave continued watching Mike. Then, as if a silent decision had been made, he spoke, "Been good. You look well. You know, you been doing a good job, but just between us boys, you better jump on that H4 repair soon as you can. John's really been riding Don's ass; he's gonna come down on you, if you aren't careful. Need help with it?"

Mike thought what a good man Dave was as he responded, "No, no thanks Dave, I can do it. I'll get on it first thing tomorrow."

"OK," Dave said, "Let's get on with this mess. I'll buy you a burger later."

The two men set about installing, or in Mike's case re-installing the equipment. Mike knew Dave quickly figured out this wasn't entirely on the up and up, but as he had hoped, he did not press it.

Late that afternoon, the two men sat across from each other munching burgers, the job completed. "Well, what have you been doing with yourself, Mike? Still collecting shells?" Dave asked.

"Oh yea, I still mess around with it, can't get too much beach time."

"Yea, you know my daughter, Tori, is a beach nut. She likes to sketch ocean scenes, birds, and such." He took a sip of Coke, "Thought she'd outgrown it, but here she is a grown working woman, spending every spare moment with all that artist stuff." He looked reflective, then said, "She sure loves it though, especially the birds. Bet she's drawn every kind of native bird."

Mike's interest perked up. "She draw any ospreys?" he asked.

"Oh yea," replied Dave, "One of her favorites, calls 'em the sea kings."

"That sounds interesting, I'd like to see some of her pictures."

Dave, busy chewing his burger, swallowed and said, "Follow me on to the house now. Tori's coming over after work, you can meet her and see her work."

Caught off guard by the invitation, Mike said, "Well, I don't know, I ..."

Dave interrupted before he could finish, "Aw, come on, you ain't doing anything. I'll give you a cold beer."

"Well, OK. Sure. Sounds good." Mike had a serious bashful streak when it came to girls, but he would like to see her pictures. Maybe she could provide more information about the osprey as well.

Several hours later, after meeting the attractive twenty-three year old and looking through her pictures, Mike joined Tori and her parents in the backyard for small talk and cool drinks.

"Dave," his wife said, "you promised to help with the tax forms tonight."

Mike stood, "I need to be on my way anyhow," he said.

"No, no," said Dave, "You kids enjoy yourselves while we go through this paper torture."

Mike glanced at Tori, who smiled at him. "Well, if Tori wants to," he muttered.

"Oh please stay. I'm enjoying your company," she said.

"Well, that settles it," Dave said. He kissed Tori on the cheek and turned to Mike, "See you later."

Finding himself suddenly alone with the girl, Mike blurted out, "Your Dad says you like ospreys." Nothing like getting right to the point, Mike thought.

"Oh, they're my favorite. They're so beautiful and independent," replied Tori.

"I was wondering what you might know about them," Mike asked anxiously.

"Why are you so interested? Are you into birds?"

"Oh no, I just hang around the beach a lot and, of course, do the microwave work. They're impressive birds, thought they were eagles at first."

"A lot of people make that mistake. They are the same family: raptors."

"Raptor! I thought that was a dinosaur."

She laughed, "No, they really are a hawk; many people refer to them as fish hawks. They don't get nearly as large as eagles, but they get big, about two feet high and some have six feet wingspans."

"They sure look like eagles, particularly from a distance."

"Yes, but if you look closely, you'll see they have m-shaped crooks in their wings and dark brown stripes across their eyes. When they're flying you can also see a dark band on the underside of their tail. They're also the only diurnal bird of prey."

"They're what?"

She laughed. "They hunt day or night. Not even an eagle does that."

They sipped their drinks, enjoying the gentle evening breeze. Mike felt very comfortable with this girl; unusual for him. Most girls he'd met seemed silly, dependent and boring. Tori was different: mature, confident and interesting.

"I see two of them together a lot," Mike broke the silence.

"What?"

"Two ospreys together."

"Oh yes," Tori responded, "They usually mate for life." She smiled mischievously. "The female is larger than the male. Maybe that's why. She also makes her hubby help with the nest building. And then when she's caring for the eggs, he does almost all the hunting."

"Where do they come from anyway?" Mike asked.

"I don't really know, but they range all over the world. I read that most of those along the east coast actually winter in South America, apparently they don't like colder weather."

"You sure seem interested," she said, studying him with curiosity. "Where have you been seeing them?"

"Oh, you know, between Vilano and Ponte Vedra where it's kind rough."

"Is that where you do most of the work for Uncle Don?" she asked.

"Uncle Don!" he exclaimed.

She laughed again. "Well, he's not really my uncle, but I've known him since I was a little girl. My Dad has worked there a long time and they fish together."

Oh man, Mike thought; Don and Dave were buddy-buddy. Now it's like a family affair. This was really getting complicated, and risky.

"Well," he stammered. I guess I'd better go."

"I'd like to see your ospreys sometime," Toni replied.

Caught off guard, his mind was racing. He really liked this girl and wanted to see her again, but he couldn't take a chance on her saying something to Don about the nest at H4.

"Tomorrow is supposed to be really nice. Do you have any free time? Maybe we could do an outing." She waited for a response.

This is terrible, thought Mike. He knew he had to pull that dish into place and hook it up tomorrow and no way could he let her see what he was up to. He sure wanted to see her though.

"Oh, I'm sorry. I didn't mean to be forward," she said. He still had not answered her.

"I, ah, have to do some work out there tomorrow with the boat, but I don't think they would like a non-company person along," he finally responded. Well, he thought, that's that. Probably killed any chance to see her again, but at least the nest secret's safe. He felt a strange mixture of relief and disappointment. Premature.

"Oh," she quickly replied, "I know Uncle Don won't mind."

Trapped, Mike thought, but then reasoned, she probably doesn't know anything about microwaves and dishes. Far as she would be concerned, he would just be doing a job. This might work after all. He could see her and get the dish up. Elated, but still worried he answered. "Well, I guess you could come out. But I'd rather Don didn't know, you know just in case . . ."

She cut him off, "That's fine. It'll be our secret. Maybe I can help with the work. I hear my Dad talking about it all the time.

Her Dad! He forgot about Dave. "Sure, maybe so," he said. "But let's not tell your Dad either, if that's OK."

She smiled, thinking how correct and cautious he was. She liked it. "No problem. Where would you like to meet, and what time?"

"How 'bout I pick you up at Porpoise Point about nine. That'll give me time to load my gear."

"Great. I'll bring sandwiches."

Mike left hoping he had not made a big mistake. Somehow, he almost didn't care. He made the scenic drive to the cottage slowly, planning the next day's job—and thinking about Tori.

The next day, she was waiting at the Point as he ran the inflatable up onto the beach. Dangling a pack in one hand and what appeared to be an artist sketch bag in the other, she ran toward him. His heart quickened as he took her luggage and helped her into the boat; obviously not necessary by the way she handled herself. She perched on the small centerboard and said with a smile, "I thought I might get a chance to do some sketching. Hope you don't mind the extra gear."

"No," Mike replied, "That sounds great."

With the H4 site barely visible in the distance, he pointed and said. "That's where I have a small job to do." He handed her the binoculars.

She studied the structure. "You must love your job, being able to enjoy all this while you're working."

Mike did not reply, again hoping this was not a mistake.

"Oh, my," Tori said, still peering through the binoculars. "That looks like a nest on top."

The moment of truth.

"It's the ospreys'," he replied.

"How neat, but I'm surprised they stay around with you working there." She lowered the glasses.

"Well, actually, I've kinda been doing the job in between her flights. There's chicks in it."

"How long have the chicks been there? You know, it takes usually six to eight weeks before they fly."

"Only a couple of weeks," he responded.

"How long will it take you to do your work?" she asked, looking concerned.

"Oh, I've already started. I just need to bolt that smaller dish down and do some quick hook-ups and adjustments, not very long."

"So you'll be through with it for a while then?"

Mike studied her, not sure how much to give away. "Yea, I think so," he finally said.

"Well, that's good. They should be fine." She seemed relieved.

"Look," she pointed.

High above, one of the birds was circling. Suddenly, it dove straight at the water, and came up with a mullet in its powerful claws.

Tori started talking, her voice was filled with excitement, "You know, they eat fish primarily, but sometimes snakes, small birds and mammals. They have a reversible outer toe that rotates to the rear of their foot when they're about to grab their prey; that gives them two big claws to grab with. Isn't that fascinating?" She was out of breath.

"Yes, it is," said Mike, fascinated with the fact . . . and Tori.

"Here's something really fascinating. Their talons are so strong and sharp that they have been known to grab a fish too large for them to lift and fly and for whatever reason, their talons won't come out."

"What do they do?" Mike asked, amazed.

"There have been reports that large fish were caught by fisherman and osprey feet were still attached."

"You're kidding!" Mike exclaimed.

"I'm not. Either the claws go into the bone and they can't remove them, or they just don't let go. A shame really, that the very thing that allows them to be great hunters and survive can actually cause their demise." She looked sad.

Mike sat silently, pondering this information. "That's incredible," he said, finally.

Tori was peering through the binoculars again as Mike continued toward the site, she said, "So what exactly do you need to do?"

"You see the smaller disc below the other two?"

She nodded.

"I need to bolt that to the pole, then splice the wiring harness to the other two discs. Probably take thirty or forty minutes, if all goes well."

"Anyway I can help to speed things up? The mama bird will probably fly away when she sees you, but she'll probably stay in the area. The less time we have to be there, the better for the chicks."

Mike contemplated the information, and her request. Finally he said, "Yea, you can probably manage the pulley rope from the boat so I can have both hands free. You'd just basically have to hold it steady when the dish is lined up with the brackets. That way I can get the bolts and holes to line up quicker."

"I can do that," she responded. "What does that dish do? Are the two large ones broken?" she added.

"No, not exactly. This just boosts the signal power. It's kinda temporary." He had cut the engine, drifting gently up to the poles. Tori, sensing his reluctance to say more on the subject, grabbed the bow rope and prepared to tie up as Mike strapped his harness on.

Mama osprey, now shrieking loudly from the nest, lifted off her perch when Mike was half way up the pole. She flew up fifty or sixty feet and began circling. Mike reached the tied-off dish and dropped the pulley rope to Tori.

"OK," he yelled. "We'll pull this in position, then you wrap the rope around the piling and hold it."

"Gotcha."

With the dish aligned, he reached into his bag for the first bolt. It slipped in easily, and he fastened it down. With the last bolt in, he shouted down to Tori, "OK, you can let the rope go and relax; it'll take about twenty-five minutes to hook up."

"OK." She dropped the rope and picked up her sketchpad.

Selecting a pencil, she began drawing, glancing first at Mike then at the two circling birds; the male bird had now joined mama.

"What are you drawing?" Mike was headed down the pole, the rolled up rope and pulley draped around his shoulders and chest.

"Just piddling," she said, closing the sketchbook, "Are you through?"

"Yep, all done. Let's go enjoy those sandwiches."

As they headed toward the shore, one of the birds soared over them and made a beeline to the nest, where it landed to the shrieking of the chicks.

"Looks like all's well," Mike said.

She smiled at his concern. "They're fine. Hope you like tuna salad." Mike ran the boat onto the shore, thinking what a great day this turned out to be.

Over the next three weeks, Mike saw Tori several times. They had seen a couple of movies, met for coffee, and had gone diving together twice. Always somewhat of a loner, particularly where girls were concerned, Mike was anxious about his growing affection for Tori.

Her zest for life was contagious and he found himself thinking about her more and more. He was, at this moment, thinking how far away tomorrow was; they were going shelling and he could hardly wait. And too, he thought, letting logic creep in, he still owed George some shells and she would be a big help finding good ones.

They shared a mutual love of ocean and wildlife, though she probably knew more than he did about both. He was learning though, particularly about the ospreys. They had gone out to check them twice, like expectant parents checking the brood. And, to his relief, the extra dish was apparently working since Don had not mentioned it again. Of course, Don was really busy with a big installation project near Jacksonville, so that helped.

Nevertheless, if he dwelt on the situation, Mike became a little nervous. He was sure Don would have his ass if he discovered the caper. Hopefully, the birds would fly in a few days and he could fix the cones, reorient the main dishes and Don would never be the wiser. With his attachment to Tori growing and her unwittingly involved, he wanted this adventure to end for his job security and more important to him to keep Tori from getting into trouble or being angry with him for not telling her the whole story. "Fly, birds, fly," he whispered aloud.

Tori arrived the next day as Mike was grabbing the shell bags from his truck. He asked if, after their shell hunt, she'd like to join him for lunch and to meet George at the gift shop. As they walked down the dunes to the beach, she accepted the invitation with great enthusiasm. With that, they set out down the beach, searching for its treasures.

Three hours later, laden with dozens of good shells, they drove into town for lunch at what had become their favorite St. George Street café. Their leisurely conversation caused them to arrive at the gift shop just as it was about to close.

"Mike," George said, busy retrieving his outdoor display as they approached. "Thought you got lost. Where you been?" Seeing Tori for the first time, he continued, "Oh, you have a friend with you today; and shells," he noted, glancing at the heavy bags. "Come on in." Look around if you like, Tori," he said after introductions had been made and Mike started unpacking the shells.

"Well, these three should take care of the osprey debt."

Tori glanced up from her browsing at George's comment, but said nothing.

"OK," Mike said. Then to Tori, "I traded for the ceramic bird you saw on my table." She just smiled and turned her attention to several watercolor paintings on display.

"Speaking of which," said George, "Did you find out how long ospreys tend their chicks? You sure were interested last time."

"Yea, I did. Tori knows a lot about them."

"Oh, I really know very little, but it is neat following the young ones at Mike's microwave site," Tori casually responded.

Mike panicked and said quickly, "Well, we'd better be going."

"So soon. Here's your money then."

Mike took the bills and hustled a surprised Tori out the door.

"Mike, what's wrong?"

"I thought we agreed to not mention the ospreys to anyone," he responded.

"Well, you didn't seem to want Uncle Don or my Dad to know, for whatever reason, but I didn't think that included everyone. What's the big secret?"

Mike calmed down. Of course, she was right. George didn't even know what he did, and Tori just thought he didn't want company people knowing she went on job sites with him—she still didn't know he was actually changing job plans because of those damn birds which put his job at risk. Man, he thought, I'm getting paranoid.

"You're right," he said, "I'm sorry. Guess I'm just a little tired. Let's go for a beer."

She hesitated briefly, giving him a quizzical look, then finally smiled and said, "OK, James Bond, but only if you stop acting so secretive."

"Deal," he responded, thinking he should tell her the whole story. He trusted her completely at this point, but still did not want to put her in the uncomfortable position with Don and Dave of being in "cahoots" with a rule breaker, or a job shirker; or whatever he was.

Oh well, he thought, with any luck, the birds should fly within a week or so and then he could do his job, not worry about getting caught, and now, more importantly, not worry about this dilemma with Tori.

"We haven't checked the nest since last Friday; want to go out day after tomorrow? I should finish a job down south by then."

"That'll be great. Let's do a picnic again."

"OK, I'll pick you up at your place at nine." Mike was ready for that beer when they arrived at the Tavern.

Tori was waiting with picnic basket and sketch bag in hand when he arrived at her apartment two days later. It was another beautiful day and Mike was excited about the prospect of spending it with Tori. They chatted over the noise of his old truck during the casual drive to the point.

"It shouldn't be too long before the chicks can fly."

"Maybe they'll be gone today," Mike responded, knowing that was wishful thinking.

She laughed, "I doubt that, but probably just a few days. You sure seem anxious about them," she continued.

"No, it'll just be good to get them out of there. I actually have some work I need to do on those dishes and the nest is really in the way."

She eyed him suspiciously. "So, is the nest causing you to get behind in your work?"

He didn't answer immediately, finally saying, "Well, probably no big deal, but I do need to do stuff." Wow, he thought, I guess that's vague enough.

"Will you need to tear the nest down to do the work?" she asked.

"No, I don't think so. Just need to turn the dishes a little. That nest is so big and well built, I think it'll be fine. 'Course there are those that would want it down so it won't interfere with the signal."

"Will it?"

"It shouldn't, because it's really above the line of sight. Anyway, apparently it hasn't so far."

"Does Uncle Don know about it?" She sized him up with curiosity.

"I don't know. Probably not or I would've heard about it."

"Is that why you've been so touchy about it?"

Her perceptiveness was disarming, but he was determined not to involve her any deeper. Their arrival at the Point saved his need to answer, "Here we are," he said instead, "Let's launch this thing," referring to the inflatable. Within minutes, they were on their way to site H4, each enjoying the calm water and mild sea breeze, their discussion now history, much to Mike's relief. However, that relief was brief.

As they neared the site, Mike could see something in the water close to the site's large piling. It quickly became apparent it was a boat. Probably fisherman tied to the posts he thought, though there were signs posted warning boaters not to tie up here. As they drew nearer to the culprits, Mike was trying to decide whether or not to advise them of their violation. There was really no harm in using the poles to tie up; it was really more to discourage vandals, or so it had been explained to him.

It was a nice boat; twenty-two foot T-top. Now, within a hundred feet of the vessel, he could see lettering on its side. His heart sank. It was a company boat! Apparently, John or Don had sent someone out to check after all. The gig is up, he thought, cutting his engine to drift along side the boat. A man in the bow, gazing through binoculars at the dishes, or nest, lowered the glasses and turned to the approaching inflatable.

Well, I've had it now, thought Mike.

The man in the boat was Don.

"Looks like you've been creative," Don said, glancing up toward the extra, smaller dish. "Would've been a lot less work to just orient the ones there, don't you think?" Receiving no answer he continued,

"Where'd you get the extra dish?"

"It's from a site we upgraded," Mike replied.

"How convenient."

A pause.

"Who helped you mount it?"

"I did," said Tori quickly followed by a defensive Mike.

"No, she didn't. She just happened to be with me when I bolted it on; I had already put everything in place. She has no part in this."

Don looked from one to the other, then back to Tori. "How you doing, Tori? Didn't know you knew this guy."

"Hi, Uncle Don. Yes, we're friends," she looked at Mike. "Very good friends."

There was a long silence.

Don nodded toward the nest. "Those birds worth your job?"

"Uncle Don. . ."

"This doesn't involve you, Tori," Don cut her off.

"I boosted the signal," Mike said

"Not to full power. Besides, you misled me, and also wasted company time."

"I planned to take care of the dishes after the birds left. I didn't think it was a big deal," Mike knew that was lame.

"It's a big deal because you had a job to do and procedures to follow, and you did neither, although I do admire your ingenuity." He lowered his voice. "You work on your own, Mike; I trusted you. Why didn't you tell me what was going on?"

Mike was dying.

"I boosted the signal. I was just trying to buy a little time." He paused. "Besides, you would've told me to tear down the nest and I didn't want to do that."

Another long silence.

Tori touched Mike's hand gently.

"How long before they fly, Tori?" Don asked.

"A week or so, maybe sooner."

He glanced up at the nest, now filled with the shrieking of excited, young birds, startled by all the commotion. He looked back at the couple in the boat, his face expressionless. Taking a deep breath, he said, "Well, I suppose a few more days won't hurt; signal ain't that bad."

Reverting back to his boss voice, he looked at Mike. "Soon as those chicks fly, you orient those discs and replace the cones." He glanced up. "May as well leave that extra dish; never can tell when you might need it." He looked back at a shocked Mike and beaming Tori, "Well, I gotta go," he said, reaching to untie his boat.

"Uncle Don," Tori said, flipping through her sketch book, "Just a second, I have something for you." She found the picture she had been searching for, tore it out and slipped it into one of the protective covers she always carried. She handed it over to Don who just shook his head as he pushed the boat clear to start the engine.

With a wave, he idled the boat away.

Just before planing up, he slipped the sketch out of its cover. It was Mike, dangling from a pole, the nest in the background, three chicks looking over the top. Soaring above, barely discernable, two ospreys in flight, and across the top, the words MIKE'S BIRDS.

Don replaced the sketch carefully in the pouch and throttled the powerful boat to full plane, letting the rushing wind flow across his smiling face.

***

THE AMAZING WALTER

Everyone hates something.

In Walter's case, he hated water. It was good for drinking and then only because it was necessary to relieve his thirst. Otherwise, he hated it. If it rained, or even hinted at rain, Walter would quickly seek shelter. And if there were puddles, he would stay put.

His dislike for water also meant that Walter never took a real bath. He had developed his own methods and version of bathing.

At the moment the sun was shining and Walter was stretched out enjoying its rays. His graceful frame was totally relaxed, in a manner that was unique to him. Occasionally, when dosing, he would twitch; particularly if the touch of water entered his dreams. Walter hated water.

That indisputable fact made his choice of where to live really strange, because Walter lived in Florida; St. Augustine to be precise, where showers are frequent and hard. He had often thought of leaving, but he really loved the Old Town. Having so much leisure time, Walter enjoyed his long stalks through the streets and alleys. There were always interesting things to see and do, and the tourists were particularly nice. Some locals had become familiar with him, sometimes speaking and providing the occasional handout.

Since Walter did not talk, someone, years ago, started calling him Walter. He didn't know why; it wasn't really his name, but it stuck. So now there were several shopkeepers, workers, and such who referred to him as Walter. Of course, there were also those who called him by other names and weren't very kind, but for the most part, he could usually avoid them.

Perhaps Walter's favorite pastime was prowling the streets at night, which, he now thought, it's time to do. With a great stretch and yawn, he drug himself up and headed back toward the Plaza where he had been hanging out earlier. Besides, he really wanted to check out the center of the park. Earlier, he was watching some city guys doing a lot of digging, but couldn't figure out what they were doing. He would have stayed longer observing their strange activity, but one of the guys, James, kept throwing clumps of dirt at him and shouting obscenities, so he finally left. Some people were just mean, and that definitely included James; strange too.

Even though James knew he was called Walter, he usually called him dirtbag or bum. He also knew Walter's distaste for water, so he delighted in splashing him every chance he got, which was frequently since James was a city employee and worked primarily down town.

Approaching the site, Walter saw that James and the other work-man had left. Strange, he thought, they left that big open trailer. As he moved closer, he saw that the trailer had been backed up to the large hole they were digging and was full of dirt. As he stood by the hole, his curiosity peaking, he wondered why the large opening was oblong. Then, to his right, he noticed a large object strapped to a loading flat. It appeared to be some sort of statue, holding a big bowl.

Wait a minute, Walter thought, it's a fountain! They were going to put water in the hole and let it run up through this object, this fountain. Walter had seen others around town. He hated them because not only was it filled with water, but also when the wind gusted, it caused the shooting water to blow on him if he happened to be passing by.

Just then, the loose dirt around the rim of the hole shifted and Walter tumbled into the hole. To make matters worse, water had seeped into the bottom and Walter found himself splashing around. Quickly, he scrambled up the side and began drying off, looking over the now swirling pit, half full of water.

Something had to be done, but what? This town, and Walter, did not need another hole full of water!

Looking around, he noticed the large trailer full of dirt had a back gate, which was latched. Upon closer scrutiny, he saw an iron lever with a spring attached on one side of the trailer. Ah ha! Walter remembered seeing the city guys use this trailer to dump rock. If you pushed that lever down, the gate opened and out would come its contents.

Walter hauled himself up on the trailer and positioned his weight on the lever. Nothing happened. Obviously, he was not heavy enough. He needed help.

As fate would have it, his friend Chelsey wandered up. Chelsey, CC for short, was big and, well, to put it gently, not playing with a full deck. But she was a good friend, sometimes more, Walter fondly recalled. This is great, he thought; with our combined weight, we can release the gate lever.

CC, more than happy to oblige Walter, her favorite beau, scrambled up the trailer and jumped on the lever. The gate opened with a great clang and the dirt went spilling back into the hole, almost completely refilling it.

Walter, feeling very pleased, invited CC to dinner, which she gratefully accepted, and together they went strolling toward one of their favorite alleys. What a lovely evening this was turning out to be.

When he opened his eyes the next morning, Walter saw CC had left. He closed his eyes, contented, then suddenly recalled yesterday. Quickly, he jumped up and headed for the Plaza. Arriving there, he cautiously approached the hole, or former hole, he thought humorously. As he got closer, he could hear James, agitated, explaining to the foreman that he knew he had shut that trailer gate.

Walter, not wanting to miss this exchange, walked right up to the edge of the filled pit and stood silently. James saw him, stared briefly, and shouted, "What are you looking at, dirtball?"

Getting no response, he turned back to the foreman, whining for him to send a crew down to help uncover the hole.

"I don't think so," said the foreman. "You screwed it up, you fix it."

"But I tell you, it's not my fault," James protested. "Somebody trying to be cute did this after we left," he yelled, "And if I find out who...." He trailed off, red faced and looked at Walter, the water hater.

"Wait a minute, you don't think that dirtball...."

The foreman held his hand up. "James, you're losing it ." He glanced at Walter, now sitting, calmly grooming himself. "How in the hell could a cat open that gate? Now get your ass to work."

As the foreman left, James turned to his new chore and glanced again at Walter. Picking up a clump of dirt, he tossed it toward the tawny cat, who nimbly dodged by jumping up on the trailer lever, where he sat and began licking his paws in a most contented fashion.

***

ZERO ONE

Strolling leisurely along the Plaza, enjoying another beautiful spring morning in the Old Town, my peaceful thoughts were interrupted as the newspaper folded under my arm was abruptly snatched away. Startled, I turned to see Flyman, pounding away with my paper at the rim of a trashcan, yelling, "Damn cursed fly!"

Oh great, I thought. Just what I needed; the local nut case. Flyman, we all assumed, was not his real name; no one seemed to know what it was, or who he was. He just showed up one day years ago and seemed to do nothing but wander around mumbling to himself and slapping at flies; sometimes actually there, sometimes not. He never spoke to another person; only mumbled to himself. I was among the many who had spoken to him, became familiar, but nevertheless, he never spoke directly to us.

Still agitated from the paper snatching, I yelled, "Flyman, give my paper back! What's your problem? Why don't you get a life, you idiot!"

" I had a life once."

Startled by his statement-his speaking, I just stared for a moment, then blurted out, "You spoke to me."

"A fly ruined my life," he said.

"What do you mean," I responded.

Flyman held my gaze, turned, gesturing at me to follow, and sat down on a nearby bench. To my amazement he began speaking. With a distant gaze in his eyes, he recounted this bizarre story.

"Years ago, the serenity of a peaceful Sunday afternoon was invaded by the distant hum of the enemy. I gave a disgusted grunt and looked toward my companion, who had already begun to unsheathe our weapons.

This madness had been going on for weeks now; always with the same guerrilla tactics; hit and run. Sometimes they came in pairs, but more often it would be just one. The lone one, Zero One, we named him, had proven to be the most awesome foe. His ability to wantonly escape our best planned, most carefully laid traps and to evade our defenses utterly devastated our morale. He came, destroyed what he wished, and created havoc in his departure. Never have I seen such flying! He had to be the most maneuverable aviator of all times. He certainly was the most sadistic because he always planned his arrival during our most off guard moments."

The Flyman paused. He was damaged in the war, I thought; that must be his problem. Something happened. But what about the flies?

He continued his story.

"This day, as usual, Zero One had chosen his arrival time well. It had just stopped raining and the gentle touch of fresh air had us both in lazy moods. I was stretched out, watching the sunlight shimmering on the wet leaves like diamonds under neon lights. My companion, smiling like a happy child, was snoozing peaceably. Suddenly, the hum grew louder."

Flyman became very excited, stood up, gazing at the sky, and continued.

"I jumped up with a grim look of determination on my face. My mind was set; this had gone on long enough. Today, Zero One would meet his doom! I glanced at my wife, who had all the weapons at the ready, and could see that she agreed. Enough is enough!"

His wife, I thought. What kind of war was this?

He was speaking again.

"The sound became deafening and I could see a small, black speck at ten o'clock. As he dived toward his first target, I lunged; but in my frenzy to destroy the green, hairy-legged invader, I instead obliterated my wife's freshly baked cake. Abandoning the chocolate coated fly swatter, I grabbed the newspaper and hastily rolled it into a crude weapon. Looking like a cave man searching with club in hand for the evening meal, I quietly prowled the perimeter in search of the bug-eyed varmint.

All at once he came zooming by my right ear. Swinging blindly, I hit the swinging, shimmering chandelier, behind which he had retreated. Over the sound of breaking glass and my wife's yells, I could hear Zero One, heading straight up at full throttle. Grabbing my shoe, the nearest weapon in sight, I hurled it with what was left of my dwindling strength. Eureka, direct hit!'

Now Flyman was speaking in a loud, excited voice, swinging his arms wildly. A crowd had gathered as he continued.

"Zero One came spinning out of the horizon with his engine faltering. I watched with a mixture of joy and amazement as his body fell through space like a leaf falling from a tree. I listened in fascination to the sound of wind rushing past his helpless wings like a speeding car passing in the night. Then, when victory was almost mine, his engine caught. I stood, in utter disbelief, and watched Zero One cheat the hands of fate as he pulled out of the dive and landed smoothly on the screen door."

Flyman paused, as if picturing the scene in his mind again. Suddenly, in a loud, animated burst, he continued his story.

"Shouting, screaming, and shaking, I grabbed for my wife's antique vase, knocking her down in the process. I hurled the vase, over the shrieks of my wife, at the fly. The vase tore through the screen, hit a porch pole, and shattered into a thousand pieces. Through my battle weary eyes I saw Zero One do two loop-the-loops and fly off. As I ran into the yard yelling at the creature, my wife ran by me, jumped into the car, and left. I haven't seen her since."

From the crowd that had grown, mesmerized by Flyman's story, a voice asked, "You lost your wife over a stupid fly?"

"Not just a fly," he responded. "Zero One is more; he's immortal. Every time I think I have killed him, he pops up again, but one day I'll get him, I know I will."

"Watch it, watch it," he yelled slapping the shoulder of a startled tourist."

"Damn it, missed again," he mumbled as he turned from the crowd and wandered aimlessly down the sidewalk.

Still glued to the park bench, I glanced around at the dispersing crowd and thought it really is a wonderful spring day in the Old Town. The sun is out, birds are chirping. And, I thought, looking at the disappearing back of Flyman, I don't have any flies chasing me!

***

LOVE IS....

The general scowled and threw his quill among the papers scattered on the crude table. "The trouble with the army today is that the soldiers are spoiled. Too many politicians, wives, and girlfriends in the mix. They're a bunch of sissies."

"Yessir," his aide responded. You could be right."

"Of course I'm right. It's not like the old days when I was young. They're like a bunch of kids now; no sense of discipline. There was a time when we would straighten them out with a good course of bread and water or a few days in the pit."

"Yessir," the aide said, recognizing the general's need to vent his frustrations.

"You're probably right," he repeated.

"Of course I'm right," the general yelled again. "If these savages down here kick our ass, we deserve it. They send me a bunch of boys to do a man's job. Why, a whole company of 'em can't even run down four Indians."

The general referred to a recent farce involving one of the garrison's companies getting lost for days in the tangled swamps of this godforsaken land; this Florida.

"Well, I don't know general," the aide replied cautiously, "Throughout history military leaders have had occasion to feel their hands were tied when dealing with their troops. Why even Washington had numerous discipline problems."

"This ain't Valley Forge and I ain't George Washington. I'm talking bout now, here, this place," snapped the general.

The aide, knowing something had prompted the general's foul mood asked gingerly, "What's gone wrong sir? Anything I can do?"

"No." Scowling at the papers on his desk. "We have to survey out four million acres of swamp to keep track of those damned Indians. Sounds delightful, huh?"

"Well sir, I guess it will take some time, but it shouldn't be too difficult."

"So I just order an engineer platoon, supported by a reinforced infantry company to the alligator, snake-infested swamps for months, or years, and tell them to map out the boundary in between raids and jungle fever. But what do you think I have to worry about first?"

"I don't know sir."

"Well, let me tell you," snapped the general. "Love. We have let too many soldiers marry, or fall in with all these prissy settler girls coming in here now, so half of 'em figure if they cry to the preachers or visiting politicians, they can sit on their ass in the garrison and get out of the real soldiers' work. Soldiers need to be dedicated to the profession and not a gingham skirt."

"But, general, love is a natural thing," said the aide cautiously.

"Bullshit! I have no time for whiners and crap that detracts from our mission!"

"But sir, don't you think that's a hard way to look at the natural order of things? And besides, surely we can dig up enough single and unattended men to complete the job."

"Of course we can, after wasting time sorting through the excuses, stupid requests, preacher involvement, and every other type of crying known to man."

He took a breath, spat out, "Love...it makes me sick! There was a time when we would have received these orders and been gone in three days."

The aide stood quietly.

"From a military viewpoint, a soldier with a family or love struck ideas is a burden and all 'round pain in the ass," he continued.

"I guess I see what you're saying sir," said the aide, "But I'm not sure I agree with you."

"Why?"

"Well, respectfully sir, but I don't believe you've ever been married, otherwise you might feel differently," replied the young aide, thinking of his own sweetheart and the day they surely would be wed.

"Oh really. Well I have news for you young sir, I have had many opportunities and accompanying desire."

"But chose not to take the plunge?"

"Never," shouted the general. "Love and soldiering don't go together; they are totally incompatible. When a trooper gives in to love, his mind slows. Show me a sentimental soldier and I'll show you a trooper who is of no use; particularly in the taming of savages in this wilderness."

"That's a bold statement, sir."

"When it comes to love," the general responded, "Soldiers should be like those Asian monks. Even thinking of love dulls the senses, which endangers not only the soldier but his fellow troopers as well. I'm sure you think that an old fashioned viewpoint, but it has served me well through all these campaigns."

"So love in any form is to be avoided?"

"Every form," the general waved his arms in dramatic fashion.

"Then sir, it will be interesting to see your reaction to this dispatch," said the aide, handing the general a piece of paper.

He then stood quietly while the general scowled over the dispatch. The aide had already read the document and knew it was higher headquarters demanding to know why the general had not hung the Indian, Chief Osceola.

The aide knew, as did many, the general's strange feeling, including respect, for the great chief, now imprisoned in the old fort.

The general had actually hired Osceola many years ago to be a tracker for his Army. The then young warrior had brought in many army deserters and found soldiers who had become lost in the murky swamps. The general had grown to admire his proud independence.

That respect had become mutual and grown over the years as battles with the savages grew more frequent and Osceola rose to become Chief of the Seminole tribe, and the two men found themselves on opposing sides. Osceola was unrelenting in his fight to keep Seminole land; he would not give up, and would not even talk about a treaty, feeling that the white man had tricked his people too many times and was not to be trusted.

And now, the aide reflected, the great chief was here, imprisoned, because this very general had guaranteed his safety if he would meet with him. The general was subsequently ordered by the visiting territorial governor to place Osceola under arrest and if a treaty was not signed within days, to hang him.

The governor left and the general, these many weeks later, had neither a treaty nor a hanging.

The brig sergeant of the guard had confided to the aide that the general made frequent visits to the chief's cell. He said that many of the conversations were simply two great soldiers recalling past events. And others, ending in frustration for the general, concerned the treaty and Osceola's refusal to discuss it.

The aide knew there was no love lost between the current governor and the general, and his silent refusal to hang the chief could easily result in the end of his distinguished career. His anguish was evident.

The general looked up. "This is pure rubbish." He threw the dispatch to the table.

The aide snapped to attention and turned to leave.

"Wait!" the general commanded.

"Yes sir."

"Does he still have the fever?"

"Yes sir, and now he's painted his face and just sits crosslegged staring ahead. When we tell him he will be hanged if he doesn't sign the treaty, he smiles and says he will die in his own time."

"Did you bring his family to see him as I ordered," asked the general.

"Yes sir, but he still won't sign the treaty. He says it is not his land, it is the land of his people, forever."

"With a company of troopers like this man, I could conquer the entire country," said the general.

"Yes sir," responded the aide, remorseful that he could not offer a solution for the general's dilemma.

"He won't ever sign, will he," mumbled the general in an uncharacteristically mild voice."

"No sir, I don't believe he will."

"Who else has seen this," he asked, pointing to the dispatch.

"Only your executive officer, sir."

The general pushed the piece of paper toward his aide. "Tear it up, speak of its contents to no one and send in the executive officer."

"Yes sir," replied the aide, picking up the dispatch as he turned to leave.

With his hand on the door latch, the aide turned back toward the general and said, "Love seems to come in many forms. Wouldn't you agree, sir?"

Regaining his composure, the general glanced up, his eyes softened briefly, over the hint of a smile, then as though remembering who he was and who the young aide was, bawled, "Get out of my face and do as you were ordered."

The aide, secretly smiling, gave the general a crisp salute and quickly departed.

* * *

THE TALENT

Charlie awoke with a start. Through his foggy mind, he had a sensation of something touching him.

"Get up old man," he heard a voice say.

Another prod in his side. He glanced up to see a cop standing over him.

"Come on, don't take all day." He now recognized the intruder as one of the St. Augustine policemen who patrolled the downtown area on bikes.

"You got some I.D. on you," the cop asked.

"You've asked me before and the answer's the same. I don't have any."

"Yea, and I think I told you before, you're supposed to be able to identify yourself."

"Oh, I can do that. My name is Charlie, which you already know."

"So you say. 'Course we don't really know that for sure, do we?"

"Why don't you guys leave me alone? I ain't hurtin' nobody."

"You're hurting me because I have to take time to get you off the streets so the tourists to our fair city don't stumble all over you. I could run you in for vagrancy. You're probably broke too, huh?"

Charlie slowly got to his feet, moaning as he did so from the stiffness caused by his bed of grass and sticks.

"I got money," he said, extracting crumpled bills from his pocket.

"Hustling the tourists, huh?" the cop said, noting the healthy wad of bills.

"Have you ever seen me hustling tourists?"

"No, but I'll catch you. Just a matter of time." He appraised Charlie's attire. "Why don't you get cleaned up and buy some clothes with that money?"

"I'm happy with my clothes, and I don't mess with tourists, other than conversation. Matter of fact, some try to give me money sometimes, and I don't take it." Charlie stated rather proudly.

"So where do you get it?" the cop asked.

"I have a talent. It gets me by."

"Oh, really," the cop replied, "And what talent might that be?"

"Well, it's hard to explain. I can kinda tell things about people."

"Ok, Charlie, take your talent and move on. Go get something to eat."

"Good idea." Charlie knew the cop wasn't a bad guy. Just doing his job keeping the streets safe for the horde of tourists that always seem to be around in the old town. "Have a good day, and thanks for the wakeup call," Charlie said, smoothing his old coat out.

The cop smiled, shaking his head. "You too, Charlie. Don't step on the pigeons." He climbed on his bike and rode away.

The beefy man was pacing around the room, scowling at the speakerphone sitting on the polished table. He glanced at his partner reclining in the large office chair, who likewise had a look of consternation on his face.

He laid the big cigar down in a brass ashtray and spoke to the speaker, "Are you out of your mind, Dennis? If this is a joke, I'm not laughing."

The other man leaned forward in his chair. "Dennis, you've done good work for us, but this is unacceptable. We told you the situation, and we trusted you to get the job done down there. We could have found a no name up here, but we used you because you're in St. Augustine and we wanted to keep things personal with the theatre folks there. I told you this was going to be their biggest play ever, and there are big bucks riding on the whole venture," he paused and started again, "And we have investors who expect to get their money, and more, back."

"I know, I know," the voice from the speakerphone said in a calm manner. "I know the play is important to these people down here and of course to you guys. I couldn't come up with a known name that was available and right for this part, but I'm telling this kid fills the bill. He'll be great. Trust me on this."

The beefy man spoke again, "We'd like to, Dennis, but this is too much. There's too much money riding on this, and the entire play revolves around the main character. If he don't work, the play don't work so the client is unhappy, the investors are unhappy, and we're in the red. It's too risky. You let us down, man. We asked you for a name for this part and sitting outside my door is this clown you sent to us who has never done any serious work and looks like the guy down at the donut shop."

"Donald, just think of all the stars that have been made on one film or play. No one ever heard of some of 'em before that first big outing and zoom, they're overnight hits. There's something about this kid. I'm telling you he can pull it off." The speakerphone went quiet.

The men in the room looked at each other, thinking the same thing; time is running out, and no leading character. What now? Go with another agent and try to come up with someone on short notice; any agent would demand a fortune to pull that off. Or take a chance.

In silent agreement, the two men nodded at each other.

"I'm sorry, Dennis. You've done great work for us in the past, but a Cary Grant this guy ain't." He reached for the speakerphone button.

"Donald, wait, wait. Listen, are you still doing that other opening tomorrow?" Dennis asked, in the calmest voice he could muster.

"Yea, so what."

"Shoot a test of the kid I sent you and show it during the milling around social before that opening. See what the audience reaction is." Dennis waited.

"What would that accomplish. We wouldn't even have time to look it over first and reshoot. Waste of money." He reached for the phonebutton again.

"Don't reshoot it. Give 'm a few lines, shoot it once, show it as a filler, and see what happens. What have you got to lose?"

"Well, Dennis, you're so frigging confident, you pay for it and we'll have it shot." Donald looked toward the other man who nodded agreement.

There was silence in the room. Finally, the phone crackled and Dennis, in a more subdued voice said, "OK, but if I'm right, give me the contract for that new band search you're about to start."

"Who told you about that?" Donald inquired.

"Hey, I get around. Come on, Donald, you can smooth this over with the money guys. What's the big deal with a little background screening during the chit chat; particularly with me paying for it."

The other man spoke, looking at Donald, "Hell, let's do it. One more day can't make matters any worse." Then to the phone, "Dennis, if this busts, it's adios between us. You understand?"

"Yessir. You won't regret it. I promise. Will you call me from the opening after the screening," Dennis asked anxiously.

"Oh, we'll call you. You just better hope for the right reason." Donald reached over and disconnected the speakerbox. The other man rose and said, "Well, set it up." He opened the door and glanced out at the kid in question. Turning back to Donald, he said, "You know this could really hurt us."

Donald, with a shrug of resignation, replied, "I know, I know. Wish I had a fortune teller that knew her stuff."

Charlie finished his breakfast of jalapeno cheese grits at Azalea's and left a generous tip. Best grits in the world, he thought. Strolling out into the warm Florida sunshine, he decided to take a walk along St. George street to see what kind of interesting conversation he could get into.

As he passed by one of the many street musicians that usually filled the streets around the Plaza, he paused to listen to the tune being played. Too bad, he thought after a while. Not bad, but he'll always just be a street player. Voice lacked that something; whatever that is. Charlie smiled to himself, and threw a buck in the musicians can.

Dennis lit another cigarette and glanced at the phone. He picked the instrument up to insure a dial tone was present. Everything seem to be working. They should have called by now, he was thinking. Is that good or bad? If it were good news, they probably would have called right away. Or, if it was bad, maybe they would have called to relieve their anger by yelling at him over the line. Or maybe something happened with the test. Maybe they didn't do it. No, surely they would have called if they changed their mind.

Before he could conjure up another scenario, the phone rang. His heart pounding, he squashed out the cigarette and picked the phone up. From the other end, he could hear only a loud commotion. "Hello."

"Dennis, can you hear me?" What sounded like Donald spoke, over the roar of an obviously large crowd.

"Yes, I can hear you, barely. What happened. What's going on there?" Dennis responded, almost afraid to hear the answer.

"This kid is great! The place is going nuts over the screen test. We're gonna sign him here before we send him back to you, that OK?"

"Of course, of course. I thought you'd like him. So, we also have a deal on the band search?" Dennis asked, hoping Donald had remembered that part of the discussion.

"Pal, you keep doing this good, and you can have any deal I got. I'll get your check and paperwork out tomorrow." The phone line went dead. Dennis reached into his drawer for a cigar, smiling.

Two days later as he replaced the phone after having confirmed with his bank that his handsome fee had been transferred to the account, Dennis reached for the overnight envelope that had been delivered from Donald's office. He ripped open the top and poured the contents out on the desk. Oh, he thought, they're making this too easy. Stuffing the contents back into the envelope, he grabbed his hat and left the office.

He hurried down St. George Street, glancing around as he went, occasionally peeking inside one of the numerous cafes that lined its streets. Turning the corner, he spotted the object of his search. "Charlie, hold up," he yelled across the Plaza to the rumpled man strolling among the tourists.

"Hey, Dennis, what's up?" Charlie greeted Dennis as he hurried up.

"How you been, Charlie?"

"Been good. Got somethin' for me?" he asked.

Dennis glanced around and moved Charlie toward an empty bench, away from the crowd. "Yea, I do. An easy one." He said, as he opened the envelope and spread several pictures of singers and bands about on the bench.

"Ah, musicians. I like that better than actors. Get a better twitch." He shuffled through the pictures, asking as he did so, "How'd we do with the young actor kid?"

"Fantastic. Oh, here's your dough." Dennis took out a wad of bills and peeled off several, handing them to Charlie. "That Ok?" he asked.

Charlie barely glanced at the money as he stuffed it into his pocket, his attention totally focused on the pictures. "Oh yea, that's fine." Culling the pictures, he finally handed one to Dennis. "That's your group."

Dennis took the picture and looked at Charlie. "You sure? Strange looking group."

"Have I ever missed?" Charlie asked, rather defiantly.

Dennis laughed. "No Charlie, I guess you haven't." OK then, I'm off. See you in few days. Charlie was already wandering back among the crowd.

As Dennis turned to go, his cell phone rang. "Hello."

"Dennis, Donald, you get the package on the band search stuff? Thought we'd give you all those that were sent in, solicited and unsolicited. 'Course the hard part is hearing and seeing them and figuring out who the next star is. But I know as always you're up to it."

"Yea, I got your stuff. Lot of work to do, but I'll shake something out. By the way, did we talk about a bonus if I find your next rock star really fast," Dennis said as he looked again at the photograph Charlie had picked, smiling as he did so.

***

Ancient City Verse

Colorful characters
Places
Secrets

Visitors

The gaggle in the Plaza.

Most wandering aimlessly,
But some with a sense of purpose,
Though known only to them.

Baggie shorts, sunglasses,
Tanned legs, maps held
Tightly, giving meaning to
An otherwise uncertain stroll.

Stops at intersections, map
Orientation; discussion,
Disagreement, decision,
Then onward, hurriedly,
Lest that next site, in place
For centuries, be gone.

Tyler

On a clear, calm night
In the Old Town bay,
Tyler, made listless by the rum,

Stumbled to the deck
And reached up to
The stars.

They were beyond his grasp,
And leaning, he fell
Into the waiting arms
Of the moon's lover

Shattering the mirror surface.
Just as it reassembled,
Tyler emerged, mind forcing
His hand toward the deck rail

While his heart begged him
Stay in the warm, liquid
Arms, but

Too late, the rail in his
Grasp, the rum beckoning.

Street People

The morning sun
Causes a stir
From bodies in
Sleeping bags or
Curled in question
Marks with old blankets.
St. Francis House full,
With these few scattered
About left to their
Own devices; to rest, survive,
Return from the night's high.

No answers, only questions.
Another day consigned
To unfulfillment.
One certainty for the
Moment; stay close,
For breakfast is nigh.

Charlie

Weathered, worn face,
Bulbous nose, ragged
Mouth fixed in a
perpetual grin
above a sunken chin.

Eyes laced with
Red-worn,
Under a furrowed brow
That resembles
A gathering storm.
Charlie.

Asking for change
But somehow not begging,
And if none offered,
A shrug, then on to the next.

Watching tourists with
A reflective gaze,
Perhaps seeing fond
Memories through the haze,
Or wondering where they
Went, the better days.
Charlie...

Carriage

Starting you is
Not always easy;
Harder on a cold day;
Reluctant, leaving a
Warm barn and sweet hay.

Once brushed, braced,
And hitched, your single
Desire is to return here;
To that end, you
Are always slightly in gear.

Your load, on wheels
Of wood and steel, roll
Freely on these hard streets,
Though you abhor stopping
Where two meet.
Your brakes are marginal,
In a perpetual state
of the near miss,
due in part to a
Foggy state of bliss.

Your ears are immune
to the constant banter
of the driver guide
imparting old city history
to those along for the ride.

Others from behind press impatiently
From their steel steed, but
To no avail, for you only
Have one speed; until
Of course, the barn is in sight,
Then those reins must be
Pulled ever so tight.

Artisans

The Old Town
Is,
Among other things,

A home to
Artisans.
Some notable,
   Most self proclaimed.

Its quaint streets
And festive
(though with demeanor)
atmosphere lulls
   the writer, artist,
   the free thinking
   into secure warmth.

All others,
Those visitors
Treading into this
   Delicate, imperfect world,
Are but a necessity
Required to cheer
The artisan,
Without thought,
Unaware of the wealth
   They have found.

Hog

It's a happening
Every year.
Like clockwork.
Just before new
Buds grace the foliage
In the plaza.
Still a nip in the air.
But sunny.
A different breed,
On different steeds,
Jarring the quiet,
Breaking tourists monotony
With a different sight.
Bandana's, levi's, leather;
Four
Or more,
To a space, kickstands
Their tether.
Hogs that roar
Instead of squeal,
High octane their meal.
Tolerated, even as old
Town buildings shake,
Middle aged tourists thinking
That's where I'd like to be;
On a hog,
In the old town,
Free.

Legion

One Anderson Circle,
Overlooking the bay,
   They gather.

Teetering on stools
Too wobbly for the unsteady,
But nothing more is offered
These stout of heart,
These warriors of old
Who have only their
   Tales to be told.

Years change the
   Events
Or perhaps only the telling.
Stories are heard often by
Those in frequent attendance.
No one seems to mind.

Cracked walls match
Faces
That reflect years unkind,
And history understood
Only by them.

War was youth
And dreams, but
Now only blurred memories.

Talk is loud,
Jokes are plentiful,
And on us.

Chieftain

Proud chief, unbowed,
Rocked with the fever
  Of his land,

But unconquered.

Brought to that great
Fort of stone
  By trickery.

No treacherous general
Could win the fight,
Even with the great
Chieftain wilting in that
  Small, damp room.

Dying in a different
Land, far away,
On his terms,
  Painted.

Still, no treaty.

Body among the worms,
Headless. His presence
Felt even now on moonlight
Nights among the
  Stacked coquina.

Great chieftain forever.

Whose griefs were many.
Whose trust was betrayed.
Whose waters still flow
Whose land and people
  Still free.

PLACES

Old Jail

Cold steel and brick camouflaged
By that wealthy railroad magnate
With stucco, in Queen Ann style.

Matching the playhouses of
Rich friends on holiday, some
Forsaking afternoon tennis to
Hear the gallows' door thump.

No view through those barred windows.
Floors and walls blank,
Causing memory and fantasy to merge.

Thoughts of escape
From that plank bed
And threadbare cover,

But failure would conjure
More indignities from
Slow-witted, ungrateful guards.

Tasteless food and rusty water
To pamper what spirits left,
Taken with emancipated reason,

Savored slowly over the
Objections of visiting mice and
Amusement of the spinning spider.

Renovation

What fascination we have
Re-making the old houses
Of the ancient city.
Workers treading cautiously
Across thin planks supported
Precariously by a woven
Tangle of iron.
Blue gauze air, laces
Of light bending through
Ancient panes.
High peaked ceilings with
The smells of times past,
Walls soaked with
Residue from countless
Cookings; blending
Of food, burning wood, charcoal,
Oil.
It's work. But love too.
Strong calves and thighs
Flicker from constant
Stooping, climbing.
Eyes sting from
Sweat, slippery tools
Hard to hold.
With the late sky
Dimming through old
Slated vents, tired
Workman snake down
The scaffolds like grey
Spiders, carefully. No net.
A dangerous business,
Re-making the old.
Preserving history.
With love.
Making old new;
  But old...

St. George Street

Every tourist who enters
The Old Town gates
Will eventually stroll
St. George Street.

They are of every size and description.

Preserving the poetry of diversity.

Persistent,
Moving ever forward,
An integral part of the
Caterpillar that is this
Mass of humanity.

Pigeons move deftly
Among feet
Unscathed,
Watered in summer
By the sweat of
Tightly packed captives.

Street smells.
Chocolate.
Displays announcing
Every souvenir possible.

New mixed with
Old; blending.
Alive.

Terrys

Images dancing in the mirror
Like rolling waves on the sea,
Bleary eyes staring back
At what is left of me.

Jumbled mind straining
To recall a face,
Moving to the urinal
With unsteady but manly grace.

Some tourists, but
If known, you are received
With more kind eye,
And grins grow even wider
When the scent of perfume is nigh.

"And did you hear this one"
says he,
"Well, even so, listen,
it's free."

Pity these fools
And their beer and wine,
And me,
Through no fault of mine!

Plaza

It's friendly
In the Plaza.
Inviting.
Even hawking hustlers
Are intriguing;
All have stories --
Some are even true.

Always in motion,
But at ease,
Like the squirrels
And birds moving
Over branches and
Through the air.

Each scene, daily,
Different. Caused so
By changing faces;
Some to never return,
Just as a fallen leaf
Cannot lift itself
To join the twig once again.

Perhaps that is the why
For friendly chatter
Between strangers;
Sharing this place,
This time,
With the fragility
Of an unbruised flower.

Imagine

I have discovered
On some Old Town streets,
Those fronting ancient
Shops and houses,
Where bricks and cobblestone meet,

Against a misty dawn,
One can imagine sights
And sounds of times past
Before manicured lawns.

Emerging from ornate houses,
Wellbrushed, mustached gentlemen
In stiff white collars
Off to their shops.

Snorting, morning sounds
Of an old horse, withers
Trembling, warming to
The day's work.

The smell of smoke
On the bayfront,
Rising from an old barrel
Warming boat workers
Huddled amongst great pilings,
Surrounded by shrieking gulls.

The haunting sound
Of a foghorn,
Announcing the start
Of another day's ritual,
Echoing through
The small streets and
Alleys of the Old Town.

On The Beach Early

Walking this desolate
Beach early, to
Only the sound of
Purity; sandpipers
And gulls feeding among
The gentle swells,
Unattentive, for I
Alone am here
With them and share
Their brief respite.

With the solitude, head
And heart venture
Into reconciliation,
Perhaps understanding.

Water foams beneath
My feet, completing its
Journey, my own
Still unfolding.

As the pattern of water
Shore bound breaks around
My ankles I feel
Sadness,
For I am the intruder.

With the sun I
Must leave this
Beach, before my
Head fills with
Portentous pettiness
That is a part of my
Journey but has no
Place here.

Bridge Of Pain

That old bridge
Graced by lions,
Struggling against
Pounding wheels,
The elements,
  And time.

The vague sea
Calmed somewhat
As the inlet
It has become creeps
Further in,
Nipping at the great
Columns relentlessly,
Year after year pushed
  By tide and wind.

Unchanged, save for
The seasonal follies
Of man when the
Great spans are adorned
With first lights, then flags,
Now banners;
  Still the same.

Adored, even when
Its rusty hinges
And grease filled
Gears force open
Its cavernous mouth
Without shame
For that distant sail,
When it becomes the
  Bridge of pain..

Outback Crabshack

If you hunger for something special
Or maybe you're just a little down,
I know a great place to go,
    Just west of the old town.

Datil sauce, strange
Critters on the wall and
Good conversations abound,
But if Miss Margaret is there
    Be prepared to hang around!

Joe will be prowling
Like a big ole' bear,
Along with friendly David;
    He's always there.
And of course Miss Jean
With that perpetual smile;
The Outback Crabshack gang
Waiting for you on that
    Little creek, six mile.

Just before the bridge
Make a right rudder,
Experience the dream that
Grew out of shoeless Cutter.
Crabs, shrimp, fish or
Steak, and those big ole' taters;
Top it off with that special
    Sauce and a hunk of gator.

No shoes, no shirt, no problem.
Always plenty of music and laughter
Spilling from that cypress shack;
Just part of the special lure
    That keeps us coming back.

SECRETS

The Other End

I know a place
Tucked away,
  Secret..

Off the beaten path,
The opposite end of St. George,
  Isolated.

Here, one can find quiet,
Out of the hustle and bustle;
  Solitude.

Shaded, calm.
Benches for rest,
  Or reflection.

An unkept old well
For your wishes,
  Or secrets.

Next to that old Inn.
The other end of St. George;
  Secret...

Lighthouse Porch

Early one morning while
Seeking solitude on the
Old lighthouse porch,
A pleasant sound
Floated into my ear;
Not yet dawn, only
Distant sounds from
The inlet.
Quiet.
My reason for being here.

I searched among the trees,
Still sparkling from dew
In the pale light, and finally,
As dawn gave way to day,
I glimpsed a small bird
Just as it fluttered away,

And with it the song.
One lone branch, the stage,
Like a conductor's wand
Swayed to and fro;
Happiness flown away
And sorry was I
It chose to go.

Sand Secrets

Write your secrets
In the sand
On the ebb
With a shell or stick,
As the tide rolls in.
    They will be safe.

The flow will take your
Secrets, tucked away
Safely, forever,
    In the endless ocean.

Butterfly

Crawl in.
Hang out
Fly away.

Like tourists
In the Plaza.

Except,
More colorful.
No schedule.
No destination.

Preference for
Brittle grass,
Not pavement;

Scented flowers,
Not shops.

Living what
We dream.

Crawl in.
Hang out.
Fly away.
   Free.

A Place On The Bay

Leave the gift shops,
Street hustlers and
Trolleys for a change of scene
Down by the bay,
A calmer place,
Natural, serene.

Find that place
South of the fish feeding
Restaurant--as far
As you can stroll
That way.

Your choice of seawall
or grass;
Sit among the old stone.
Watch the lights fade.
Hear the inlet murmurs.
Feel the sea wind.

With the last light
Of evening,
When washing sea sounds
Become a gurgle,
You'll be happy you
Sought out this place.

Mask

Tourists, strangers all,
Pass with a glance,
A nod.
Appraising.
Causing me to think
How better we could see
If we wore masks.
The eyes could gaze,
A voice to enlighten,
But no face
To thicken the haze.
Beauty of skin
May or may not be there
To distract those
Who would stare.
No judgment on first sight
For the mask sheds no light.
To know the person
Would be the task;
To sort out what
Is behind the mask.
To hear, to feel.
To sense what is real.
No beauty, mole, or scar;
Then truly others
Could see who we are.

Casa . . .

People watching
Is a matter of location
In the Old Town.
For those who partake,
Many places abound.

Several locations
Come to mind,
Some obvious,
Some hard to find.

Filling the criteria
To see who's who,
And a great cup
Of warm brew

Is a place of which
I am particularly fond,
Right across from
That dancing, concrete pond.

You can sit east or
West on its ornamental chairs
While others dwell within,
Up and down
Thickly carpeted stairs.

Wonderful snacks, served
By ladies with accents.
Check it out, after Flagler,
You'll be glad you went.

Plaza Solace

Solace is temporary
In the Plaza
But worth even
A brief respite.
Be aloof to the
Street sellers;
Glance instead
At birds dancing
In circles, converging,
Chasing, then flying
Away, disappearing
Into the sky.
The hustlers will think
You strange and
Move, mumbling, to
Other targets,
Leaving you with
Your bench and
Nuts for the squirrels.

Early On St. George

I walked alone down
St. George Street early, before
Dawn and the opening
Of shop doors
   And heard soft voices
   Mixed with the clank
   Of armor and clopping
   Of hooves on cobblestone;
And passed on,
With the sound lodged
   In my head.

Sparrows

Those small birds
Hop nervously
About the bricks
Of St. George
Pecking at crumbs,
Quarreling
  Or playing
Over matters of interest,
  With purpose,
  Avoiding the feet
Of those of us who,
  Though wiser,
Walk amongst the
Fluttering feathers
Without direction
  Or purpose.
Are there tourists among
  The birds as well?

ABOUT THE AUTHOR

Randy Cribbs, shown below with Murphy, is the author of 'Were You There?' and several poems and articles in various publications. He holds degrees from the University of Florida, Pacific Lutheran University, Jacksonville State University, and is a graduate of the FBI National Academy. He resides in St. Augustine, Florida where he teaches and writes. For more information, visit our website at **www.somestillserve.com.**